the last fine summer

Also by John MacKenna in Picador

a year of our lives

JOHN MacKENNA

the last fine summer

PICADOR

For Caitríona Ní Fhlaithearta

First published 1997 by Picador

an imprint of Macmillan Publishers Ltd
25 Eccleston Place, London SW1W 9NF
and Basingstoke

Associated companies throughout the world

ISBN 0 330 35213 X

A CIP catalogue record for this book is available from
the British Library.

Typeset by SetSystems Ltd, Saffron Walden
Printed and bound in Great Britain by
Mackays of Chatham plc, Chatham, Kent

the last fine summer

Last night, for the first time in weeks, for the first time since you died, I dreamt. I've been wanting to dream. I believe in dreams and in the life that goes on inside them. Not some fantastic otherworld but a place where those of us left behind can regain our sanity. And so I waited, I knew, in the end, those dreams would come. And with them would come hope.

And yesterday I had an intimation. I was driving back to Castledermot, from Athy, on the long straight up to Kilkea bridge. It was late evening and the road ahead, at the bend for the bridge, was washed by light, an orange half-light, an angle of rainbow buried like an axe-blade in the field at the river. And I knew, once I saw it, that my dream was coming, that my life would heal. But when I dreamed, it wasn't of you. It was of Kevin Bracken. Kevin who's been dead since eighty-four, the last fine summer before this one. But I was glad to dream at all and glad to dream of the dead because the dead hoard hope for me. Kevin and Jean. Dead lovers. My lovers both. And if I dreamed of him I'll dream of you. That much I know.

Where there's death there's hope. That's not just some half-clever turn of phrase. It's the truth. I don't know if you and him live on somewhere, in a heaven or a hell. I doubt it. But I know you wait to surprise me, in dreams.

And it's appropriate, if that's the word, Kevin turning up like that. I intended to tell you about him. Him and me, but I never really got around to it. And there he was, like some John the Baptist arrived to prepare the way for your second coming.

*

I have an image of Kevin's father. It was the evening after Kevin's funeral. I came up the lane from our house to his. Not for any special reason, simply to walk up to his lane, to be where he had been, to cross the fields that were his fields.

When I got to the gate of their farmyard, I saw a fire blazing in the orchard. Kevin's father was sitting on a granite roller that had lain abandoned, smothered by weeds, for years. He sat with his back to me, his saggy suit deep blue against the flames. Beyond him the wooden sheds with their tattered roofs, the one good loft protected by sheets of plywood nailed with rolls of felt. The double doors of that shed were open. He had dragged out the accumulation of years, cement bags, dry-lime bags, plastic manure sacks, anything that could be moved had been piled in the orchard and set alight. And in among the sacks and bags and rubbish, like a body folded over on itself, were all of Kevin's clothes. And Bracken sat there, watching the flames licking and drenching the laden, moss-covered September branches. Sat among the ruins of twenty years of farming and eighteen years of his child's life.

And I stood watching him, perplexed by this sudden, dramatic act of a man whose only contacts with his son had been the vicious beatings he'd inflicted through the years. And perplexed by the sorrow I felt for someone we'd both despised and hated for so long.

But I was eighteen then and guilty, still half in love with the dead boy and despising myself. I saw nothing that could ever release me from that guilt. If anything made me pity the old man it was the thought that I was every bit as guilty of cruelty as he'd ever been. He at least had been open about what he'd done. He'd never pretended to be something he wasn't. That was all I knew. And he had made this pyre, just as he'd stood that morning with his daughter, Hannah, at the open graveside. By right. Kevin's father, good or bad.

But I had no right to be there. I had no right to show my face at all. Nothing I had done entitled me to be there. And Hannah, did she have a right to be there? She stood at her father's side and faced the rest of the village across the unshut grave, as though by right as well. But if they didn't know, I did. I knew it all. Knew how much responsibility lay on us. I'd felt it when I shouldered Kevin's sealed coffin. It weighed me down in the narrow aisle between the pews, in the hot churchyard, in the gateway of the graveyard as we manoeuvred among the headstones. And even now, with the weight six feet below us, it didn't lift and, I thought, never really would.

*

It wasn't the first time I saw you. Of course it wasn't. I have no clear recollection of that. How could I have, one of a hundred new kids in a school where I was new myself. Back in my home village to teach.

'You're mad,' my father said. 'Who'd want to teach in the town where they grew up?'

But jobs were hard to come by in eighty-eight. I was twenty-two. I was full of belief and conviction. I had high hopes for myself. And high expectations of the things I could do. So what if this was my home town? All the better, all the better for all of us.

You must have recognized that. All of you. You must have seen the difference, the enthusiasm I brought to everything I did, in and out of school. Wasn't that why I got on well with all of you? Most of the time. Wasn't I the one you all relied on? Wasn't I your friend and weren't you all mine? I was the one who drove you everywhere, organized things, couldn't see no as an answer. I was the heart and soul of that year, your year, and the years that followed.

But I can't say I remember you any more than I remember the rest of that fresh young class. I look at the photographs now. The smiling boys and girls. You among them. There near the back. Always competent. Always polite. That's as much as I remember of you then. Apologies.

You'd laugh. How often have I heard you laughing, telling me I didn't deserve you, telling me you had your eye on me all that time?

'Lying with a smile,' I'd say. And you'd laugh again.

'I'm telling you, I had you in my sights. I was a precocious twelve-year-old. I knew I just had to bide my time until you noticed me.'

And you did. Up to that night, four years on. I remember that night. I've chosen that to cling to, through everything that's happened since. That night in ninety-two.

The end of another school hop, another night over. The last slow dance. I couldn't say I remembered what song was playing but you told me afterwards that it was Leonard Cohen.

'"Light as the breeze",' you said. 'Appropriate for cradle-snatching.'

When you said things like that, you reminded me of him, of Kevin. The same cynical streak.

But I do remember the rest of it, clearly. I was standing at the top of the hall, chatting to another teacher, and two of you came up and asked us to dance.

'Why not,' he said. 'It'd be rude to do otherwise.'

'No obligation,' you said.

'We'll dance,' I said. 'I'm not getting into a debate about it.'

And we moved out into the throng on the floor. You looked at me and smiled.

'You didn't mind me asking?'

I shook my head.

'Why should I?'

'I just thought . . .'

'I'm honoured,' I said.

You drew back your head for an instant and looked me in the eye. The shapes and colours from the projected light drifted across your face and hair. You seemed so serious. As though the weight of the world was on you. So serious. And so beautiful. The first time I'd noticed. That sober gaze. And the light went on drifting, brighter, darker, softening your face, shadowing your eyes, changing your hair from chestnut to red and all in a couple of seconds. And then we were sucked into the crowd and your head was pressed against me, your arms around me. Music. We were carried by the slow surge of the crowd around us and I put who I was and where I was out of my mind. I lost myself in everything that was you. Musk drifting up from your hair. Your loose shirt brushing the back of my hand. Our bodies touching and not touching. Promise in everything. Everything unsaid. You were a whisper and I wasn't sure what the whisper said or if I heard at all.

'You weren't listening,' you said when I told you all this much later.

'To what?'

'To the song.'

I listen to it now. I sit in the kitchen, at the window, looking out over the young orchard we planted, and listen and I'm back there, drinking the incense of your hair and the promise of your body almost touching mine, of your skin beneath that shirt, of your hands on my back, of your body.

Your body. Laid out in the morgue, the kiss of death on your skin, the graze of death on your temple, the blank light of death on the closed and purpled lids of your eyes. Only your hair was still alive, pillowed about you on the frozen marble of that temporary bed.

Your body. In my bed. My body inside yours. The hardness of life. Your body hard and vital, holding me. Arched against me, holding, fucking, keeping me that instant longer, the moment more, keeping, holding, touching and, then, not touching. My mouth caressing your forehead, my hands in your hair, on your shoulders, holding, holding for the moment when you tighten finally about me and suck me down inside you and I come.

Your body on the dance floor, years ago, before this curious hunger and strange death. Sometimes that's the best part, the time before it all became possible, the time when you were beyond me, when I was still your teacher and you were still my pupil. The time in the school hall when I didn't know for certain what was happening.

'You thought I was a pricktease?' you said.

'No. I don't think I knew what to think. I wasn't sure what I was hearing. It's like I told you.'

'But now you know.'

'Yes.'

'And you miss the virginal sixteen-year-old!'

'I just remember the uncertainty, the anticipation.'

Your body. That close to mine. Never closer and never more out of my reach. Not even now, not even after death.

I never wanted you more than that night three years ago. In the minutes we were dancing and in that other moment when we stood in the coldness of the epileptic fluorescence and you smiled, again, and thanked me. That instant while my hand stayed on your shoulder and your eyes refused to surrender.

*

Kevin and me were born the same month, same year, in houses at opposite ends of the same lane. We went through school together. Our mothers died within eighteen months of each other. I was nine when my mother died. We were ten when Mrs Bracken died. Kevin was always a nutcase, long before her death. Right from the word go. Always a messer.

I remember, when we were eight or nine, a summer day, and his father sent us for three bottles of lemonade. One for Kevin, one for me and one for himself. We cycled into Castledermot, bought the lemonade in Copes and started back for home. Once we were out of the village Kevin got off his bike and opened one of the bottles. He took a long mouthful.

'Here, you have some.'

'I have my own,' I said.

'So have I, this is my father's.'

'And what's he going to say?'

'Fuck him, he'll never know.'

I drank from the bottle. It was half-empty. Kevin took it from me and pissed into it until it was full again.

'Fuck them all.'

That's the way he was. We gave the bottle to his father.
I didn't stick around to see what happened but Kevin did.
He sat with him, in their kitchen, drinking from his bottle,
watching his father drink from his. He didn't care. Sometimes, looking back on it, I think he half-wanted to be
caught or, worse, he really meant it when he said he didn't
care. Maybe there was nothing he feared at home because
that was his way of not getting hurt beneath the skin. For
the rest of it, he got beaten regularly. I never understood
how he took it. He'd know it was coming, for days the
threat would hang there like a branch waiting to fall and
Kevin always seemed to want to be under it when it did.

'You don't know 'cause you never get hammered,' he'd
say. And he was right. I never got beaten at all. Once or
twice I'd been grounded but no more than that. For Kevin
being beaten was only part of it.

I remember times, we were ten or eleven, when he was
locked in the shed all day. I remember, twice, after we'd
done something crazy, like staking out some of the town
kids, naked, in the sun for a couple of hours, his father
thundering across the yard and lifting him bodily inside
and dropping him in a bath filled with cold water.

'You shouldn't take it,' I told him.

He shrugged. 'It's better than getting my head belted.'

Once, I said something about it to Hannah. She was a
year older than us. But she just shrugged, too, the same
way he'd done.

'He's not the only one.'

11

'But not as bad, not as often.'

She shrugged again and walked away.

But sometimes it was okay. Sometimes we went for weeks on end without trouble, without getting caught. We'd nick cigarettes from MacEvoys; shit in shoeboxes and wrap them up in brown paper and leave them on the roadside, just to watch people stop their cars and pick them up; pile dustbins against someone's door in the village and then bang the knocker and run away. We were wild but Kevin was a step beyond me. I worried. He didn't care. It was all nothing to him.

'I don't have to worry,' he'd say. 'I have them sussed. They can only get you if you care about them getting you. Like my father cares. He cares that I don't give a fuck about the farm, that I can't wait to get away. He wants me working on it, the rest of my life. I don't give a shit about the farm. Finish school, do well enough, get out.'

We were fourteen. He had it all worked out. Knew exactly what he wanted and what he didn't care about.

'So what do you care about?'

We were sitting in the cinema in Carlow, waiting for the Saturday night picture.

'Getting on all right, getting enough money so I don't have to worry.'

'That's it?'

'What else is there? What do you care about?'

'Same as you. But I care about my old man, things like that. People.'

'Me?'

'Yeah. We're mates. Kind of like brothers. Aren't we?'

Later, cycling home, when neither of us could see the other's face he said: 'I do care about all that. And you. And Hannah.'

He laughed but his laughter was uncertain.

I said nothing. We cycled on a bit and then he said: 'We are kind of like brothers, aren't we?'

'Sure are,' I said.

He laughed, again, this time loud. 'The Shoebox Shitters. That's us.'

Suddenly his bicycle light shot ahead of me, wheeling up the bank at the roadside, sweeping back across the black tar and crashing against a garden-gate.

'Do you know what I'd love to do?' he asked, picking himself up.

'What?'

'I'd love to piss in the teapot, the way we did with the lemonade, watch the old bollocks drinking it. That's what.'

And he did and his father found out and beat him to a pulp. He came down to our house. My father was out. I helped him peel his shirt off. The blood was still running through it, slopping in our kitchen sink, puddling the floor as it dripped from his back.

'You should go to the doctor.'

He sneered.

'Just sponge it off my back. And go easy. Okay? Just go easy.'

'I will,' I said. 'But you should do something.'

'Like what?'

I had no answer so I finished sponging him and he lay on his belly on the kitchen floor. There were four wide welts across his back and, at the end of each, the print of a belt-buckle. I dried them and then I went to get him another shirt. When I came back Hannah was at the door.

'He says your tea is ready.'

'He shouldn't do this,' I said.

'Have you got any talc, powder, something?'

I nodded.

'Get it.'

She shook it across Kevin's back. There was a tenderness about the way she did that. Something particularly gentle in the way she watched for a reaction.

'Leave the shirt as loose as you can. Don't tuck it in. And just keep out of his way and keep your mouth shut. Okay?'

They went down the lane together. I watched them from the kitchen window. I felt like crying. I remember that. I felt so sorry for them. I looked at the bloody shirt in the sink and felt desolate. I wanted things to be different for them and, so, for me, but I didn't know how to change anything. And that was it. I knew that was just the way it was.

But it wasn't always like that and it wasn't like that all the time.

Sometimes Kevin brought the madness on himself. For days and weeks he would be fine and, then, out of nothing he'd pick a fight or get himself into a situation from which there was no escape. Mostly it was with guys in school, guys who were willing to let it pass. Once or twice, at school dances, he got involved in something, came on heavy to someone big and thick, someone he didn't stand a chance against. Most of the time one of the teachers or some of the other fellows who knew him well would get him out of it before any damage was done.

It was amazing how little damage he suffered over the last two years in school. I'd try to talk to him about it but his answer was always the same.

'They're thick fuckers.'

I'd agree with him but I'd try to point out that he might as easily avoid them as confront them.

'Why should I?' he'd say. 'If you were in the situation, I wouldn't expect you to. You don't live your life on the run, neither will I.'

'But you don't have to be on the run. Just keep out of their way.'

'Not me,' he'd say.

It became a kind of catch-cry with him.

But, like I said, mostly he got away with it.

The worst time was in a schools' football final, about a month before our exams. We were playing a crowd from Dublin. Kevin was in the backs, he was doing fine, getting the better of his man. And then, late in the game, when we had it won, one of guys on the other team fouled one of our fellows. He was booked and everything was settling down but Kevin ran the length of the field and jumped on the guy. And he was out of his depth. Four or five inches smaller, two stone lighter, but he traded punch for punch, until the referee and linesman pulled them apart. They were both sent off but Kevin wouldn't let it rest. He followed this guy, walked down the sideline, blood streaming from his mouth and nose, to where he was standing, and took a swing at him again. All he got for his troubles was a badly swollen jaw.

I didn't ask for any explanation. I knew there was no point. But the PE teacher did.

'They think they can do what they like,' Kevin said.

'Who does?' the teacher asked him.

'The likes of him.'

'You're a month from your bloody exams, he could have killed you.'

'Would you say that to the others, if they went for him?'

'Yes I would.'

'I don't think you would. And I won't let it go. Not me.'

Afterwards I tried to reason it out but it didn't make too much sense.

'I don't have to put up with this shit, you know.'

'It wasn't your shit to put up with.'

'Yes it was. Fuckers like that think they have you. They look at you, size you up, think they have you in a slot. But it's not like that. I won't be put in a fucking slot by them or my father or anyone. Not me.'

'I don't follow.'

'How would you?'

And that was that.

*

*Sometimes I'd catch your eye as I came into the room.
Sometimes I'd turn and my eyes would light on you. I was
lost, totally desperate and wildly optimistic. Was that
extra button open on your blouse to tantalize me? Were
you avoiding me in the corridor? Why were you sitting in
the front desk when you'd always sat near the back, was
this another come-on?*

*I stopped you, on the way out of class, and asked why
you'd moved. You blushed.*

*'There was no room. I was last in, that was the only
desk they'd left. Honestly, sir. I wouldn't have sat there
otherwise.'*

*So did they know, the others? Had you told them
something? Was there something to tell? Was I being set
up? I doubted it, considered it, dismissed the idea. Not by
you. So why were you avoiding me? Were you running
from the consequences of that one dance? Or was it out of
your mind already? A dare you'd set yourself, a good
turn you'd done me, shaking my set ways? Were you
already gone from me, sitting down in the Laurels with
some young fellow from your class, lying in the shelter of
the gravestones in St James's, was I as wide of the mark
as my imagination could lead me?*

*There was a kind of permanent, nervous energy about
me. I couldn't walk the corridors anymore without hope
and dread in equal measure. I couldn't cross the yard at
lunchtime without suspecting love and derision. I couldn't
go down the village for the papers on a Sunday morning
without confidence and futility at my heels. I'd hear the*

doorbell and listen while my father spoke to the visitor, hear him call my name, come downstairs in the expectation of your face in the doorway. It was that crazy. I was that crazy about you, for you.

And then, one afternoon, I found myself driving a car full of students back from some debate and your face was in the mirror. Your face. Eyes that were green or blue, I couldn't decide. Hair wisping and wrinkling across your forehead. Eyes I tried to watch without being caught. Forehead furrowing whenever you laughed. No more than that.

And I read so much into your being there. You'd chosen to travel in my car, to be with me. You were there by accident, by chance. You hadn't had the opportunity to sit in front, beside me, though you'd wanted to. You had no choice and, stuck with travelling in the car, you'd opted for the back seat, as far away, as inconspicuous as possible.

See? I was incapable of anything. Of hope, of doubt, of anything, as far as you were concerned. And I didn't even know if you were concerned and didn't dare to ask. What was I supposed to do? Stop you in the street and say: 'Sorry, but since you danced with me at the school dance I've been wondering if your being in my car with four other students means you're in love with me because, you see, I'm in love with you. Or think I am.' Was I supposed to write you a note? I did, of course I did. Sat in the staffroom during a free class and wrote to you, couched my enquiry in vague terms, tore the letter up, rewrote it *late that night, more straightforwardly, went the whole way and rewrote it, again, and burned it because I saw the possibilities. At best, shock. At worst, sniggering in a corner of the girls' toilets and, inevitably, word getting back to the principal's office. All there, all those possibilities and all on the whim of a five-minute dance.*

But it wasn't a whim. Whatever else, I knew there was nothing whimsical in it for me. This was the true terror of being in love.

Perhaps it would be easier to explain, if I'd been you and you'd been me. Sometimes, when I think back over the last three years, and this last summer in particular, I imagine how much easier it might be to recreate the moments of intense intimacy that I live by. Easier to remember you inside me than me inside you, easier to feel the warmth of seed rushing in than of seed flowing out. That's not the all of it but it is a great part of it, the times on the verge of loss. The times when loss was everything – loss of control, of caring, of everything. The shuddering shattering of fucking you.

And that was there, even then, as I drove you and the others back from the school debate. It was there, more or less, in everything I did. That waiting to know, needing to discover how you really felt.

It was there the second time you travelled in my car.

Sitting beside me. Three others crammed in the back seat, coming home from a play in Dublin, dropping them off along the way, until there was just the pair of us. In the warm car, the rain suddenly trembling on the wind-

screen, caught in the oncoming lights, then swept aside. Darkness, warmth, the musky smell I depend on for my sense of you. I was as frightened then as I'm warmed now by that scent.

I drove slowly, as slowly as I dared.

'Do you want to talk?' you asked.

'What?'

'Sorry, I thought you might want to talk. You dropped all the others off first, I just thought you wanted to talk to me.'

'I do but I don't know what or how much to say.'

'Neither do I.'

Why should you have? You were sixteen, I was twenty-six; you were the pupil, I was the teacher; I was the one who should have known. But I didn't.

I stopped the car in the gateway of a field outside the village.

'I don't know,' I was mumbling. 'I've been thinking a lot since that night, the dance and that but maybe I put too much store by it. It was just a dance, you know. That's what I keep telling myself.'

I laughed because I could hear how badly this was coming out. 'I'm thinking that maybe I made too much out of that, got it out of proportion, started reading things into it. I couldn't get you out of my mind. And then I thought you were avoiding me in case I did read too much into it.' I paused and looked ahead of me, the rain stuttering across the glass of the windscreen, the night outside, you and me in the car, everything possible and, in the end, perhaps nothing.

'We should go, talk another time when it's easier, your parents will be wondering . . .'

I started the car and pulled back on to the road. You were silent. We drove through the village and out your road.

'You could have dropped me earlier, it would've made more sense.'

'Yes.'

'So why didn't you?'

'I like you being here.'

Again the silence. Driving slowly, knowing the chance was slipping away.

'I think I'm in love with you,' you said then.

I felt myself drain of energy and then, immediately, I was filled with energy again, a different kind of energy. In love with you, not I love you but I'm in love with you, the phrase branding itself in my head. For ever.

'Maybe I'm not supposed to say that.'

'You are, yes you are.'

I wanted to keep saying that, to repeat it, shout it, laugh it.

'I know this is going to cause all kinds of hassle, the school thing and everything, I do see that.'

I nodded. 'We need to talk. Find time to talk.'

We drove on. I noticed the radio was playing, too low to hear anything other than the fact that there was music somewhere in the background. We turned into your roadway, the lights of your house ahead.

'And what about you?' you asked, as I slowed the car outside your gateway.

21

'Me?'

I turned to look at you as the car eased to a stop.

'Me? I've spent the last few weeks trying to find the courage to say what you've said. Don't ask me how I went through four years not really noticing you and then lost my head in five minutes, it doesn't make sense, but it happened. I've written letters to you, torn them up. I've been afraid I was making too much out of that one night. That's how I feel. Stupid that you had to say it. And brilliant. In love. Does any of that make sense?'

'Mostly the last bit,' you laughed. 'I thought you'd never get to it. Like you said, we have to talk.'

'But this isn't the time. You'd better go in.'

You nodded.

'I'll see you in school. We'll work out a place.'

You opened the door and the light came in.

'You could write to me,' you said. 'And not tear up the letter. I'd like that a lot.'

'I might. I will.'

'And thanks for bringing us to the play.'

The door closed, you were running through the rain, across the gravelled yard, your coat over your head, into the pool of brightness outside the front door, stopping in the porchway, waving.

'I love you,' I said, out loud.

*

'My father bought an ass yesterday, to keep down the thistles in the low field. The lazy fucker, too busy with his time to look after the land and he thinks I'm going to row in and look after it for him when the exams are over. He has his shite.'

'It's just an ass,' I said.

We were sitting in the loft of the Bracken's barn, the high warm, dry, dusty loft of what was a ramshackle building of wooden cladding that had been called the barn for as long as anyone could remember. It was early summer, eighty-four. We were three days clear of our exams and three days ahead of summer work.

'The best days of your life,' Kevin said. 'The days between school and college.'

'You're sure you did well enough, aren't you?'

'Absolutely. I worked my balls off for the last two years, even when the rest of you were dossing I never drew breath.'

'I know that.'

He nodded. 'Well now the chickens will come home to roost and I'll pluck their feathers and fly away.'

He opened his palm and blew onto it. Motes trembled and swarmed in the sunlight.

'Just like that. Here and gone.'

'You shouldn't build too much on it, you know. I'm not, not until I see my results. Just in case.'

'No sweat,' Kevin laughed. 'The work is done, the reward will be reaped, the grant will be mine and I'm up and out of here and he can buy another ten fucking donkeys to do his work. And christen them.' He leaned closer to me, beckoned melodramatically.

'Do you know what he tried to do, he tried to rope me in. When he arrived back last night, with the ass in the trailer, he called Hannah and me out to look at it in the yard. And he turns to me and says: "Have you any idea for a name for it, Kevin?" The fucker, he never bothered naming a dog in his life and he starts this arse-licking. But I had him. "Call it Hote," I says to him, straight-faced. "Fair enough," he says. "Hote it is. Now, will you drive it down to the low field for me?" And I did. Drove it down, saw it settled. Donkey Hote.'

I sniggered.

'At least you got the joke. He didn't, never will. The cunt.'

'You have the summer to put in with him,' I said.

'I'll do that. I'll put it in. I'll do everything I'm told. He thinks I don't see why he's eased off the heavy stuff, why he doesn't try to beat the shit out of me anymore. He thinks I don't see all that, the way he's trying to ease me into liking what he has laid out for me. The fucker thinks I don't see any of it. And all the time he doesn't know I have him sussed. I'll be the perfect farmboy for the next seven weeks and then I'll show him the exam results and I'll wave the grant cheque under his nose and I'll be gone. And then it'll dawn on the bastard exactly what he missed. And exactly how much I hate him.'

He smiled but there was an edge to the smile, a twist on his lip, the kink I imagined in the smile of a killer. The sunlight was pouring in through the slatted timbers of the barn, throwing a blind across his face. But each time he moved, each time the light caught his eyes it reflected as it would off a flat stone. There was no room in there for anything but blankness when he talked about his father. It unnerved me. I'd seen it before, many times, but I sensed the blankness thickening, the hatred setting, the room for escape shrinking.

'Do you know what we should do?' I said.

'What?'

'We should go down to Keatley's field, go down to the river, take a few jam jars and catch pinkeens, the way we used to when we were kids.'

'That's a brilliant idea. Genius.'

That's the way he was, in anything that didn't concern his father, totally open. I was never afraid to suggest anything to him, no matter how crazy it seemed, even to me. He wasn't like the others in the class, they'd dismiss something like that with a sneer. But for Kevin there was always a possibility, even if it was only of recapturing a taste of something we'd done ten or twelve years before, something as childish as paddling in two feet of water, chasing tiny fish with glass jars, releasing them when we were done with the game. He didn't care what anyone thought. But, where his father was concerned, there was no room for change. For manoeuvre, yes, the kind of manoeuvre we reserve for dealing with those we don't really want to deal with at all. But for anything else, definitely not.

I didn't blame him but neither did I fully understand him. I had only some small idea of what he and Hannah had gone through but she, at least, had cut their father from her life, even though she lived at home. But not Kevin, his father's will dominated him in a way he couldn't see. He was so intent, so set on escape that he couldn't see that I watched him clowning about and I wished that was all there was to him, that and our friendship, but I knew there was too much more.

He turned in the saddle and waved.

'Donkey Hote!'

*

You didn't wait for me to write. On the Monday after that trip to the theatre, on the Monday after a weekend when I thought of calling to your house on some pretence, on the Monday after a dozen rewritten letters that I dared not post, your letter came. It was there when I got in from school. There on the kitchen table with two or three other letters. I opened it first because I knew the handwriting. Opened it with real fear. I suspected the worst, as I've always done. Presumed this was the end. I imagined the phrases: 'thought better of it'; 'wouldn't work'; 'cause problems for everyone'; 'it's not that I . . .'

I had it all mapped out in my head, all the reasons why not.

I took the letter up to my room, in case my father came in, and sat on the bed we were to lie on so often afterwards, the big bed that dominates that room. The afternoon outside was nondescript. As it should be, I thought.

I unfolded the letter. One foolscap page from a school pad.

And then I read it.

I'm not sure how to start this letter. I could say Dear Sir but that doesn't sound right. I don't even know what to say. Well, I know what to say but maybe not how to say it or how much I should say here. I was really glad you drove me home after the others last night because at least we got to talk. Not enough but some. I wanted to talk to you for a long time. I even thought of writing to you a few weeks back but I wasn't sure what to do. Anyway, I was really glad about last night. If the Easter holidays came and nothing was said I'd have gone really mad. I kept thinking about that. Two weeks away from school and maybe not seeing you.

I don't know what will come of this, not much while I'm in the school I know. I do know that. And there's two years of that – I know!

Is it too far to think ahead or have we to think that far away? I'm not sure.

I told you I wasn't sure what to say or how much. I haven't said anything really but I just wanted to write. I hope we can talk soon.

Lots of love,
Jean xxx

I read that letter a dozen times, sitting there at my window, dredging every sentence for more.

I wanted more. I wanted everything, then. After the months of uncertainty, despite your warning that things would be difficult, in the face of everything I knew, for those minutes, while I read and reread the letter, I wanted everything. I wanted you there, in my room, in my bed. I wanted your light body on mine.

I allowed myself that straw because I knew I couldn't allow it again in the foreseeable future. There'd be nothing like that in the two years ahead of us, the twenty-six months until you finished in the school. I knew all about the romantic nonsenses, the gymslip fantasies but the reality was that we couldn't afford anything like that. One mistake and we'd be hung out to dry. And no coming back. I'd made such a mistake once and learned the lesson well. Not now. Not again. Not with someone I loved. And did I love you? Was it just a fantasy? A twenty-six-year-old fantasizing about a sixteen-year-old? The old, old story?

I didn't think so. It had never happened before, not to me. I went my way, did my job, never looked at any of the kids. I didn't even chase anyone from the village, I always kept my private life elsewhere – Carlow, Athy, Dublin. I was careful about that. I couldn't be accused of being a uniform-chaser. This was something else. Something that had blown up in my face the night of the school dance, something that hadn't gone away and I hoped never would.

And, while I sat there and the dull afternoon dripped away beyond Mullaghcreelan Hill, I thought about Kevin and Hannah and me. All that love spilt carelessly, all those aimless feelings, all that intimacy scattered like wasted seed across the ground. That's how it seemed. That's how it had been. And I was determined not to have it happen again.

I waited until my father was home and we'd eaten.

'I'll be out for a while,' I said. 'I have to call to a couple of the kids, some school stuff.'

'No trouble I hope.'

'No, just routine. I won't be late.'

He liked to know. Not where I was but whether I'd be in at ten or twelve or three. Once he knew, he was happy.

I drove down through the village. Already it was dark. Out to your house, rehearsing what to say.

Your mother opened the door.

'Hello, Mrs Duffy. I was looking for Jean, there's some stuff I wanted a couple of the transitions to look over with me, could I borrow her for an hour and a half?'

It all came out like that. I'd probably have gone on talking if you hadn't appeared in the hallway behind her.

'I was wondering if you could spare an hour or two, some stuff that I wanted to go over, some survey stuff I have to get off in the post tomorrow?'

'Course she can,' your mother said.

'I'll just get my coat,' you said.

You went upstairs, I heard the tap running. When you came down your breath smelled of spearmint.

'Thanks.'

'Anytime. And drop in for a cup of tea when you get back.'

'Right.'

'And your father is keeping well?'

'Great.'

'Good, sure we'll see you later then.'

You were already standing at the car, laughing.

'I didn't put her up to it. And it'll only be a cup of tea, she won't be quizzing you on your intentions.'

We sat into the car.

'How come you're so much more relaxed about this than I am?'

'Am I?'

'Seems that way to me.'

You shrugged.

We drove out past Levitstown, across Maganey Bridge. I stopped the car and turned off the lights. You rolled your window down. The Barrow was snoring a field away.

'I like that sound,' you said. 'I like the sound of water.'

'I'll make you a fountain.'

'Is that a promise?'

'It probably is.'

I smiled at you, your face like a ghost's in the dusky light. I should have known there and then, should have sensed it, shouldn't I? But I didn't. My only sensation was the need building inside me, the need to talk and tell. The need to hear you tell me how much you loved me. The need to store up everything because this hour would be all there was until God knew when.

'We have a screw loose, haven't we?' you said, softly, seriously.

'I got your letter.'

'Yeah, but did you read it?'

'At least a dozen times.'

'And?'

'And I wanted you, there and then. I wanted to hear your voice, I wanted to touch you. Want to . . .'

And I did, I reached out and touched your shadowy face with the back of my hand. Your breath whispered against the skin on my knuckles, the wind came in off the river. Everything was absolutely still except for the breathing of the wind and your breath on my hand.

There was so much to say, so much to catch up on but I knew, we both did, that those minutes of almost silence were more important. I know that now, that the silence is not a thing to be feared. I listen to it, I hear you breathing through it. Your breath comes back to me, back from the banks of the river, from the darkness. Your breathing tells me you're there. Not that you're alive but that things live on. Photographs, odds and ends, tee shirts, a pad you sketched rough plans in. All these things are to hand, so why shouldn't your breathing be there too? Soft but definite. Not so soft that it might be imagination, not so definite that others might catch it and wonder at what's going on. But there, genuinely there.

Like what? How do I explain it? Like the scent of a river, that definite scent. You can walk a river a thousand times and never catch that scent but it's there and, once you know it, you'll always recognize the water, from three fields away, from a gateway on the road, at night. There's always that something that says river, that names the particular water. Just as there's always that something that whispers you.

You see how difficult it is to explain all this?

Impossible to do anything more than scratch the surface, knowing that no one will understand fully, not even those who have some idea of what I'm trying to recount. Impossible to do and impossible to avoid the attempt. It's there like a touch, like memory and need and then there's the knowledge that nothing will ever ease it and nothing can ever make it go away. It demands acknowledgement, deserves attention. It's all as vague as a late afternoon reflection that's uncertain but oddly undeniable.

That's why I'm waiting for the dreams of you, waiting for the sound of your voice again. Words, hesitations, intonations, the paraphernalia of your life.

Paraphernalia. That was my favourite word for all the bits and pieces you left about the house. Things that brought softness to a house that had been without softness for so long.

Is that too much to wait for? I hope not.

*

Most of the time Kevin's madness was controlled. The viciousness was saved for his father and even then it was mainly inside his head or on his tongue. The rest of it had always been fairly harmless. There were the times in that last school year when he seemed to lose control, like that football match when he'd gone looking for trouble, the times when he courted aggression for no good reason.

But, early that summer, something else broke through. The weekend after we'd finished our exams we went to a dance in Athy. We were hanging around outside the hall, kicking about, wondering whether it was worth going in at all, weighing up the limited alternatives. And then, out of nowhere, Kevin was in a fight with two other guys. It seemed to me it had all blown up out of nothing. He'd wandered away from me to where these guys were standing beside a car. One minute he was talking to them, the next he was wrestling with one of them and then the second joined in. It was all over in thirty seconds, they didn't hang about, just lashed into him with fists and boots, did their damage and ran. There was little to see and nothing to hear but Kevin came out of it with his forehead cut and his face badly bruised.

I got him away, took him down to the river and washed him up as well as I could and then we sat in the porch of the courthouse, waiting for the time when Hannah and her boyfriend would pick us up.

'What the fuck was that about?' I asked.

'Dunno.'

'Come on, Kev, you're not talking to a teacher, you're talking to me.'

'It just started.'

'Yeah.'

'I just said I fancied the red-headed guy's girlfriend.'

'What girlfriend?'

He shrugged.

'They were just talking about some girl. I said I thought

she'd be a good ride. He asked me what I was talking about and I said I thought she looked like a ride.'

'And you don't even know her?'

He ignored my question. 'He said to piss off or he'd kick my head in and I said I still thought she'd be a good ride. That's what started it.'

'Are you fucking mad? You know what these animals are like, they'd think nothing of cutting your head off and throwing it in the river.'

He smiled, his face was green in the street light, his eyes already puffing from the beating they'd given him, his lips an ugly blistered line, but he was smiling.

'They could have killed you.'

'I don't think so.'

'Well I do. And for what, what's the big deal about getting your eyes closed and your mouth battered? Explain that to me. Tell me, maybe I'm thick.'

'Because we're the Shoebox Shitters,' he said weakly.

I looked at him and I didn't understand. This guy who'd just put his life on the line for no reason was on the verge of tears. He was throwing out a phrase that we'd used half a dozen times in the last four years, a phrase that meant little to either of us and I didn't understand it but I did know it was intended to bring some saving grace to the situation.

'Yeah. We are. We're the Shoebox Shitters but we don't have to shit in the boxes while these apes are still trying on the shoes.'

He laughed quietly.

'Let's pick our time and place. And the next time, give
me a warning, okay Kev? So I can be up and running.'

He nodded, his head between his knees, his eyes out of
the light.

When Hannah and her boyfriend came to pick us up
she wanted to know what had happened.

'A disagreement,' Kevin said. 'But it's sorted out now.'

She seemed to be too busy arguing with the boyfriend
to make any more of it.

We didn't go back to any dances in Athy that Summer.
But that wasn't the all of it. The following Friday Kevin
suggested we go to a disco in Carlow.

'And no big stuff,' I said.

He grinned.

'No big stuff, no fights. Just women.'

'And not someone else's women?'

We came out of the discotheque at half one in the
morning. We'd drawn a blank.

'I nearly shifted the one with the blue top,' Kevin said.
'Only that her brother was waiting to bring her home.
Only for that, I'd have been away in a hack.'

The crowds were streaming out of the hall and we were
standing twenty yards from the door, directly across the
road, watching for someone who might give us a lift home.
Suddenly, Kevin flung himself at a telegraph pole, his legs
wound around it, pretending to screw it for all he was
worth.

'Ah fuck, she was a ride, I'd have got the ride. Course
and distance winner. I'd ride and ride and ride her.'

At first, I laughed, as did the people passing by, but Kevin didn't stop, he went on, banging himself against the pole, his pelvis thudding harder and harder against the wood, his arms clinging to it, as though he was drowning, his face pushed against the rough creosote. People had stopped to see what was going on, stopped to laugh but the laughter didn't last. Something wasn't funny anymore and they drew back from Kevin. A circle opened around him and everyone kept their distance. He'd stopped shouting, all we could hear was the thump of his body against the pole and then the quieter, more sinister sound of his cheek razoring the splintered wood as he slithered to the ground.

I stood with the crowd, knowing I should do something but afraid. Afraid that he'd lash out at me if I tried to stop him. I stood there till, finally, he was finished. His body a withered heap at the foot of the pole, his arms still loosely round it.

'He's drunk,' someone said.

But he wasn't drunk.

When the crowd began to lose interest and drift I went and knelt beside him. One of the bouncers from the discotheque came over to where we were.

'Is he okay?'

'Yeah.'

'Woman trouble?'

'Something like that,' I nodded.

'Maybe you should bring him back inside, wash his face,

it looks a bit rough, his mother won't want him coming in home that way. We won't be locking up for a while yet.'

We hefted Kevin between us, half-carried him inside. I sat him on one of the toilets and pulled the splinters from his face.

The bouncer came in with two cups of coffee.

'It's not worth it, sunshine. No one is. Let her go.'

Kevin stared at him. I don't think he had any idea what the bouncer was talking about.

'I'll talk to him tomorrow,' I said.

'I've seen it before. Fellas getting their lives tied up in knots over young ones that don't care one way or the other. And young ones throwing themselves at fellas that you wouldn't spit on.'

Kevin stood up.

'We better go.'

'You're all right?'

'Yeah, thanks for the coffee and all.'

'Yeah, thanks, thanks,' I said.

'Talk to him,' the bouncer said.

'I will.'

And I tried. We walked home from Carlow that night, didn't even try to hitch, walked the seven miles. There was a full moon and the sky was sallow and hot, it had a blue plastic tint in it. We were silent till well past Knocknagee. I was the one who broke that silence.

'What's going on, Kev?'

'Nothing. Nothing's going on.'

'Is there something at home, worse than usual?'

'No. I'm working my bollocks off. He's happy. I'm waiting. Five weeks left.'

'Are you worried about the results?'

'Why should I be?'

I lost my temper. 'Come on,' I shouted. 'A week ago you got the shit kicked out of you in Athy, tonight you knocked the shit out of yourself and you say nothing's going on. That's madness.'

'I was taking the piss, I was horny.'

'Bollocks.'

'Okay, I'm a spacer.'

'Well do your spacing with someone else, not with me, I don't need that.'

I strode ahead of him. Once or twice I looked back but the distance between us was stretching. Coming over Barn Hill I looked again and he was just a form on the roadway, a quarter of a mile behind. A black figure on a white night. I wanted him to mean nothing to me. I wanted to go home, get into bed, sleep until midday and get up and lie in the sun, forget all about this carry on. But there was too much there to forget, too many years together, too many times when one or other of us dragged the other into trouble and neither one ever walked. The only difference here was that the trouble was more serious because it was coming from the inside and I didn't feel I had what it took to deal with it. But then neither did I feel I'd walk away.

So I sat on the gate of the pitch and putt course and waited. The night was breaking up over Fraughan Hill, light slithering across the sky. Any minute now the sun would appear. Any minute now Kevin would come over the brow of the hill. And then he was there, trudging along, head down, the dawn lightening his hair, his shirt loose outside his jeans. Down the hundred yards to where I was sitting.

'You have to talk to me, Kev, now or later. Talk to me or we're dead.'

He didn't look up, just nodded his head.

I jumped down off the gate.

'We'll go and make some coffee in my house.'

'Yeah,' the word was a whisper.

'You okay?'

'Yeah.'

It was broad daylight when I opened our front door.

I plugged in the kettle and then went upstairs to my father's bedroom.

'No lifts,' I said. 'We walked all the way.'

'You should have rung me.'

'It was good exercise. Kevin's downstairs. I'm making coffee, do you want a cup?'

'No thanks. You're all right then?'

'Grand.'

'Good.'

He turned away, his face to the wall, and he looked so small in the bed, so alone.

All of them, I thought: my father; Kevin; Kevin's father, probably. I felt sorry for them but I didn't include myself. I was fine.

Kevin was sitting at the kitchen table; he'd made the coffee. I opened the windows, heat flooded the room.

'You'll be shagged, waiting tables in this weather.'

I nodded.

'When are you starting?'

'Monday.'

'What shift?'

'Eight to four.'

'Could be worse.'

'This is bullshit,' I said. 'You're stalling. Now, what's the story?'

'If it was as easy as that I'd tell you, wouldn't I?'

'Kevin, I don't mind you going mad, I like it, you were always a looper, but last night was different, last week in Athy was different. I don't want to spend the summer being afraid to go anywhere with you, not knowing when you'll blow up or what you'll do or who you're going to take on. That kind of stuff isn't funny. It frightens me.'

He was silent.

'I was never afraid of you, ever. That was the great thing, always, you were looney but there was never a reason to be afraid. In the last while that's changed.'

He laughed, a short laugh that came out like a sigh.

'It's not just getting out of here, you know. Not just getting away from the old bastard down there.'

He waved towards the lane, there were tears on his cheeks, tears at the corners of his mouth, tears running down his chin, tears mixed with the scrapes and cuts where I'd pulled out the splinters from the pole.

'Sometimes it's not enough, you know.'

'What's not enough?'

'Hate.'

He drew in a huge sob and then his breath came out like death. He swallowed and looked at his fingers, picking at one of his nails, trying to control his breathing.

'Kevin, I don't give a fuck, you know. It doesn't matter. I've seen your father beat you up and down the yard, I remember you being thrown into baths of cold water, I know what went on, remember. I can handle all that. But I can't handle the last week. It's like being with someone totally different. Someone who changed just like that.' I clicked my fingers and he looked up. The sun was on his face, his eyes wet and red, his skin pocked and cut.

'Jesus, Kev, this was to be the best summer ever, best days of our lives. You said it. So tell me.'

'What do I say?'

'Say whatever you want.'

'That I thought if I shouted loud enough about riding I'd get this out of me, if I got that girl last night, got her shirt off, felt her tits, I'd be all right or if I got my head kicked in over some young one in Athy I'd be the same as the rest of you.'

'I never realized I was just one of the rest.'

'But you're not like me either.'

'Meaning?'

'Meaning queer. Bent.'

'No, I don't think so.'

'What are you saying?'

'That's all I'm saying, that I don't think so.'

My coolness surprised me. I wasn't shocked, just intrigued. This was something new between Kevin and me, something deeper than the sexual sweepings we'd hoarded, haphazardly, over the years.

'I'm saying I'm glad you told me. It doesn't change anything.'

'Okay.'

'And I'm saying you don't have to go on proving things to me or anyone else. The kind of stuff you're doing doesn't prove anything, you know.'

'Okay. Maybe I can tell myself that too, that I don't have to prove anything. To me.'

We sat at the table for a couple of minutes.

'Do you want some more coffee?'

He shook his head.

'No, I'm jacked. I better go home.'

'I'll call down when I wake,' I said. 'We'll cycle out to Mullaghcreelan, talk and stuff. Okay?'

'Okay.'

*

We spent so much time, in the first months, being careful, ensuring no one could have the slightest idea about what was going on. If we were back again wouldn't we do it differently? Wouldn't we take the chances when they came instead of making a difficulty out of every opportunity?

We talked endlessly about what we mustn't do, setting traps for ourselves, so effective they almost caught us for ever. It seemed like joy wasn't allowed in our company. Our conversations were strained and when we parted we congratulated ourselves on how austere we'd been, persuaded ourselves that we were filling a reservoir with love and sensuality and that when the time came, and you were finished school, it would wash away all the frustrations. And so our lives would go on. As if we can talk of life going on, as if we can separate one day from another and our lives from the lives of the people we love. As if tomorrow is a promise that will be kept. I should have known better, shouldn't I? I should have learned by then.

Once, earlier this summer, one evening when we were in the orchard, I said that to you but you put your fingers on my lips and stopped me talking.

I was lying on my back in the long grass and you were lying on your stomach, beside me. Even then, I sensed how much time we had wasted, how foolish I'd been to dam up the love that was there.

'It's all right, we have it now, it's not going to go away,' you said.

I waited until you took your finger from my lips.

'But what was I waiting for?'

'We were both waiting. It's not lost, you know. None of it is lost. It was just time, maybe we needed time to get ourselves ready for each other. We don't know, do we? All we know is that it came out okay?'

Your wrist was close to my eye, its skin as taut as the skins of the young apples above our heads, the colour of the earth.

I remember you as a brown girl.

Once, I walked down the orchard in the late afternoon, when the heat of the sun was bearable, and came across you lying naked in the grass, half asleep, the dry stubble grass angled under your long legs. And I stood there while your body spun all kinds of shades across the yellow grass. Bronze, brunette, bay, auburn, chestnut, sorrel, hazel, roan. Your skin was smoke in the burnt orchard.

I knelt down beside you and opened my palm on your shoulder. Your eyes stayed closed but your mouth creased into a smile.

'I wish we'd fucked, all the times we could have,' I said.

'We can, now,' you said. 'For now and then.'

'It doesn't work like that.'

You rolled onto your back, a smudge of dry earth across your right breast, lighter than the colour of your skin, and opened your eyes.

'Well then, Mr Pessimism, we'll do it just for now. And tonight we can do it for the future, we can begin storing up, for when you're too old to do it.'

I remember you laughing, not all that long ago, in the rainless orchard where the fruit is almost ripe now.

*

'Is young Kevin all right, are things smooth enough with his father and himself?'

My father and I were sitting at the kitchen table, eating our lunch.

'They're okay.'

'If there was anything you thought should be done.' He hesitated. 'If you thought things were any worse than ever they were, I could have a word with his father. We always got on well enough. He might listen to me.'

'No, he's okay. It's just after the exams and all, he's just on a bit of a run, y'know?'

He nodded.

'He's lucky to have you, to have a friend that good is something.'

'And he's a good friend to me,' I said.

My father nodded.

I was tempted to ask if I was as good a friend to my father as I was to Kevin, to ask if he needed a friend the way Kevin did, but it wasn't something I could do then.

'If there is anything, any way you think I can help out, you only have to say. You'd do that?'

I smiled at him and nodded.

'Yes, I'd do that. And thanks for saying. But I think he'll be okay.'

'Will he do well enough at the exams, to get to university?'

'You can count on it.'

'Then the pair of you will still be together.'

'That's if I do all right.'

'You will. You have your mother's brains.'

It was the way his voice dipped a little when he mentioned my mother. It was that kind of moment that you only expect late at night, a moment of particular intensity, a moment when all the silence of the previous years rears up in your face. Everything might happen, anything might be said, terrible sadness might be uncovered. A moment that says this could be the day and the place when we stop pretending nothing was lost when she died. When we lay our loneliness on the table and admit to what we've gone through, separately, through all those years. But we chose to postpone the moment.

Instead, my father leaned across the table and poured tea into my cup and then into his own.

'And your looks,' I said finally.

He glanced at me and smiled.

'How could you go wrong?'

We didn't get to go to Mullaghcreelan Hill that afternoon. Instead, we spent it clearing the sewerage pipes in Kevin's yard. We stood in the heat, stripped to the waist, ramming the rods along the clogged pipes, sweating in the full burn of the sun, the water gurgling and spitting in the shores. Kevin didn't talk much, just the occasional curse or shout across the yard when we unblocked another bend on the pipe.

A couple of times I saw him wince as the sweat ran into the cuts on his face.

It took us four hours to get the system working again. We were soaked in sweat and shit by then.

Kevin's father arrived back, just as we finished. He'd collected Hannah from the shops.

'A nifty job,' he said.

Kevin gathered the rods and ran them under the outside tap.

'Yeah. You shite, we clean,' he muttered.

His father said nothing.

'You might as well stay for your tea,' Hannah said.

I nodded.

'Go up and have a shower, I'll get it ready.'

We went up to Kevin's room. He found a clean pair of jeans and a tee shirt for me.

'I'll thrown your jeans in the wash, get them back to you tomorrow.'

'Thanks.'

'I don't know why you have to come down here and spend half your day dragging pipes, if he'd keep an eye on the septic tank we wouldn't have to end up in shite to the eyes. Wait till he has to do it himself, it'll be coming out on the floor before he stirs. Bollocks.'

'It doesn't matter,' I said.

We were sitting on Kevin's bed, drying ourselves.

'Beats walking up Mullaghcreelan, doesn't it? If you had the choice between an afternoon stroll and cleaning shite from the pipes wouldn't you opt for the pipes, no contest!' Kevin laughed.

'You're all right, after last night?'

He nodded.

'Tell you what, after tea, we'll go down the back river for a swim.'

'Okay.'

We went downstairs and sat at the table with Hannah and their father. Kevin seemed to come alive then.

'How's the chap?' he asked Hannah.

'What chap?'

'Your man with the car, the guy you spend your nights arguing with.'

'On the verge.'

'That was quick.'

'Not quick enough.'

'Was he not?'

'Shut up,' Hannah said.

'Are you hurting?' Kevin asked, clutching his shirt and bunching it over his heart. 'Are you really hurting inside, is your heart bleeding like the broken-hearted, is your life dripping away, running down the drain?'

'You should know,' Hannah laughed. 'Did you see any sign of it out there today?'

'Today was shit. Tomorrow we'll look for the signs of heartbreak and heartache.'

'Well let me know. You let me know,' Hannah said, turning to me. 'If you see my broken heart, let me know.'

Her eyes were wide and bright, the same eyes that I'd seen in the photograph of her mother that hung in their sitting room.

I smiled and nodded.

'So, is he gone?' Kevin asked.

'Let's say – going, going . . .'

'He seemed a nice enough young fellow,' her father said.

'Try tying him to a harrow, see how he does,' Kevin laughed drily. 'Put Hote and himself together.'

I thought Kevin was going to go on, push things too far so that his father would spit something back at him. But they sat glowering at each other in silence.

'And when are you starting work?' Hannah asked me.

'Monday.'

Are you looking forward to it?'

'I suppose. Yeah.'

'At least you'll get paid for clearing up other people's shite,' Kevin said.

'If you want a fight then pick it somewhere else,' Hannah said. 'I want to talk to Tim, it's not often I get the chance, so can I do that, is that okay with you?'

Kevin was silent, avoiding her glare.

Afterwards, I sat in the yard, on the windowsill, with Hannah, waiting for Kevin to find his swimming togs.

'They just piss me off, the two of them,' she said. 'When one of them is quiet the other is trying to stir it.'

'I suppose.'

'What happened to his face last night?'

'What did he tell you happened?'

'He said he fell into bushes.'

'That's what happened.'

I waited for her to say something but she didn't speak.

'How's work?'

'Same as ever. This week, correction, this month it's shirts, blue denim shirts, sixty-six million, six hundred and sixty-six. Roll on the holidays.'

'I'm sorry about your man, things not going well.'

She looked at me, squinting into the sun, putting her hand to her forehead so that I could see her eyes again.

'I am twenty, you know. I'm not washed up yet. You're not that far behind.'

I blushed.

'I didn't mean it like that.'

As I spoke, Kevin came out of the house. Hannah stood up.

'Well enjoy yourselves, children.' She rubbed Kevin's hair. 'You okay, little brother?'

'Piss off.'

'Poor baby. See you, Tim.'

'What a shithead,' Kevin said.

'She's okay. She's just messing.'

We cycled down the lane, through Castledermot and out the Barrack road. The sun was still pasted high above the Mill Pond, sweating in our faces. We cycled hard, not speaking, pushing on to get to the river before the water cooled. We left our bikes at Kelly's and crossed the field to where the Lerr split, half-lolling in the pond, half-dammed to make a swimming place at the back river. The river bank was well worn, there were sweet papers and empty

cans thrown in the ditch but the place was deserted. We
changed quickly and jumped into the clear, slow river,
swimming with the slight current, down to the sluice gate
and then back again, towards the Rocks, to where the
water grew too shallow for swimming. We did this a dozen
times, moving lazily through the water, passing each other
in mid-stream. Finally, when the sun had slipped a little,
we climbed out of the water and dressed.

'We should do this more often, specially if there's no
one around.'

'Yeah.'

'I hate it when there's twenty kids fecking around in the
river.'

'We used to do it,' I laughed. 'I can remember you
running along the bank and jumping in with your eyes
closed and tough luck on whoever got in your way.'

'That's a long time ago,' Kevin said. 'I was mad then.
I'm all grown up now, amn't I?'

I didn't see too much of Kevin in the week after that
swim. The once I went to his house he was away with his
father, collecting cattle from the mart. I was getting into
my work, getting into the run of the hotel, sussing out who
was pleasant and who wasn't, doing what I was told and
putting a few things on the backburner, reasons why some
people were to be trusted and some weren't. It didn't take
too long to work out who would diddle me out of tips and
who wouldn't. I said nothing, just waited, knowing that
what went around came around. The way I looked at it,

I'd be there till late September, long enough to get my own back on anyone who tried to get at me and short enough to put up with what had to be put up with.

The best days were the ones on the early shift, cycling to the hotel just after half past six in the morning when the countryside was delirious with birdsong and the sun was already well up.

Starting that early also meant I was finished by four and out of the place for the best of the day.

I didn't like the work, waiting on people who never knew or cared you were there. Busloads of tourists who had no idea where they were, eighty or a hundred of them trudging into the restaurant together. The racket of their conversation, the get-me-this-and-that, the kitchen doors swinging in and out, the top-heavy trays of steak and croquette potatoes, seven dozen trifles and seven dozen coffees in three minutes, the same busload trudging out.

'Clear! Clear! Clear!'

The headwaiter at the top of the restaurant. 'I'm bollocky Bill from over the hill, says bollocky Bill the sailor-oh. The animals are loose, now clear the debris.'

And then the next busload and the same routine.

Sometimes four sittings in three hours.

'Clear! Clear! Clear!'

But I knew I'd survive. It was just a job and the work was concentrated. As long as they kept me on the early shift I was happy. The thought of coming in at four and being there till one or two in the morning didn't appeal to me.

'That shouldn't happen,' the headwaiter told me. 'Most of the night-staff are women who want to work late, it suits them. You'll be hit for the odd Saturday wedding, that's about it.'

And that's the way it was.

'You can get used to almost anything,' my father said. 'I wouldn't like it myself but it's handy enough.'

And it was. One week down, eleven to go.

Cycling to and from the hotel, that week, I thought a lot about what Kevin had told me. I wanted to talk to him again but I wasn't sure how to do it.

'Any word of Kevin?' my father asked.

We were having our dinner on Friday evening.

'Haven't managed to catch him all week. I might drop down tonight.'

'I saw himself and the father bringing cattle down the low farm at lunchtime.'

I nodded.

'He could make a go of that place if it was worked well.'

'Who?'

'Kevin. If he got his hands on it.'

'I don't think so. He doesn't want it. He's set on going to college.'

'Ah, I know that, but when he's finished there, when he has that done, he might want to come back.'

I shook my head.

'I don't think so, once he's gone that's it.'

'If it was handed over to him.'

'Even if his father was dead and gone, he still wouldn't

take it. He hates the place. It's just a job for the summer, as far as Kevin is concerned.'

'Is it that bad?'

'Yeah.'

'Its a terrible pity to see it gone that far. If his mother was alive it wouldn't have happened, she would've kept his father in check.'

I said nothing.

'That bad,' my father said again, very quietly. 'That's a shame.'

After dinner, I cycled down the lane to Bracken's. The yard was empty. I left my bike at the gable end of the house, propped against the other bikes that had been there for years, rusted high-nellies that had been eaten by rain and frost and sun until they were no more than skeletons of metal and rubber, without chains or saddles. As I rounded the corner, I heard shouting from the kitchen. Kevin's voice. I couldn't hear what he was saying. I stopped, waiting for him to finish but the shouting went on. I thought of turning and going home again. While I stood there, undecided, the voice stopped, in mid-sentence it seemed to me, but the silence was only momentary and then I heard a dull sound and I knew immediately what it was, I'd heard it here before, the sound of a boot buried in flesh, a dead, sinister thud, one of those sounds that you hardly hear and yet it makes the hair stand up on the back of your neck. And then it came again, followed by the slap of a hand on skin and, finally, Bracken's voice, high and hard.

'Fucker, you deserve nothing. You're good for nothing. Put up to me in my own house would you?'

And, before I could turn, Kevin was in the yard, on his hands and knees and his father's boot was smothered in his ribs. Neither of them saw me. I was frozen where I stood. And then Hannah was at the door, screaming.

'Stop it, for Christ's sake, stop it, you'll kill him.'

'He has it coming, the bastard.'

Hannah turned and saw me.

'Jesus' sake, Tim, stop him.'

Bracken spun around.

'He had it coming. No father has to take that from his children. Your father wouldn't take it.'

And, suddenly, the yard was almost silent again, just the hoarseness of Kevin's breathing where he knelt on the ground outside the kitchen door. Everyone waiting for what would happen next.

Hannah was the first to move, she pushed past her father and knelt beside Kevin. Bracken turned and went back inside. I followed him, I didn't know why but I did. He was standing in the kitchen, his palms laid flat on the table, as though supporting him. His back was to me.

'I don't think you should do that to Kevin.'

He didn't answer.

'He's okay, you know. He's okay.'

'You don't know the half of it,' Bracken said, without turning. 'Would you call your father a bastard and fucker and wanker to his face? Would you? You would not. And your father wouldn't take it, wouldn't have to take it. Never.'

'He's okay, Mr Bracken, when things are quietened down.'

'Aye, when he's out of here and gone with what he wants. He thinks a big job is the be-all and end-all. Well, we'll see, by Jasus we'll see.'

Hannah came back inside.

'He's gone,' she said.

Her father said nothing.

'He took your bike, Tim. His own is in the shed if you need it. He just took it and went.'

Bracken turned then and went through the hall, we heard his boots on the stairs.

'What was that about?'

'I don't rightly know,' Hannah sighed. 'It started about cattle and stuff and I left them at it. When I came back downstairs Kevin was screaming at him and then my father hit him, you saw the rest.' She smiled, wanly. 'What's it ever about?'

'It'll be better when Kevin gets away, when they're not in one another's hair all the time.'

'If they don't kill one another in the meantime.'

''Course they won't.'

'I'm going to walk into Castledermot. Are you going up the lane?'

'Sure.'

She went to the foot of the stairs. 'I'm going into the village. Do you want anything brought back?'

'No.'

She sighed again and came back into the kitchen.

'He'll lie up there on his bed for the rest of the night. The world and its mother could walk in here and take the place and he wouldn't stir.'

We went out into the yard.

'Jesus, Tim, look at the weather, the best summer I ever remember and this madness is going on all around me.'

I shrugged.

'You better take his bike, in case you need it. Are you working tomorrow?'

'No.'

'Haven't roped you in for weddings yet?'

'Not this weekend.'

I took the bike from the shed and we walked down the lane. There were dog-roses rearing across the gateways.

'I love this lane,' Hannah said.

She stopped and pulled back some leaves.

'See that? Do you know what that is?'

I shook my head.

'That's Rose Campion. When I was a kid, I used to think I'd like it for a name. Rose Campion, sounds better than Hannah Bracken, doesn't it?'

'I don't think so.'

'Thanks.'

We walked on a little and she stopped at a gate and pointed across the boggy field to where it fell away to the river.

'They're Yellow Flags,' she pointed to the flowers in the

shallows. 'There's all kinds of stuff along this lane, Scarlet Pimpernel and Ox-eye daisies and Milkwort and Field Scabious.'

'I never knew you were interested in that kind of stuff.'

'Didn't you, now? What did you think? That I was only interested in cutting out shirts in the factory and dancing the night away? Sometimes, I think, you and Kevin forget that I have a brain as well as a body. Would I be right?'

'I just never really got to know you as well as Kev, that's all.'

'That's what I'd like to do, be a botanist.'

'And why don't you?'

'How can I? I didn't bother working in school and I can't see my father coughing up the money to send me anywhere. Kevin learned the lesson from me. If you want to get out then you have to get a grant. I didn't spot that one coming. That's the way it goes. Maybe someday, when my father dies and leaves us the farm, if I can wait that long. And I doubt that. I think I'll have to catch someone with money in the meantime. What do you think?'

'I'm sure you could.'

She smiled.

'Are you? Do you think I have the looks?'

'Yeah.'

'Do you, really? Do you fancy me?' she laughed.

She let me flail in my embarrassment for a moment.

'No, don't answer that. It's okay. But maybe I will, maybe I'll hook my life to a passing millionaire. And then you'll miss me.'

We walked on along the lane, me pushing the bike, Hannah twirling a stick in her fingers.

'I don't think we ever talked this much before, did we?'

She looked at me. 'No, I suppose we didn't. Are you enjoying the riveting conversation?'

'Don't keep taking the piss, Hannah. You're just like Kev, always turning things around.'

'It's how we survived.'

'But you don't need to keep it up all the time.'

'Habit. But I'll try.'

'Do.'

We rounded the bend, in sight of home.

'Kevin might come back to your house, he might want to stay there till it all blows over. Ring me if he does, I'll be in by eleven.'

'Okay.'

We stopped at the gate to our garden.

'I hope you find your millionaire,' I said.

'You do, don't you.'

I nodded.

Hannah reached out and put her fingers against the side of my face. They were warm and dry and they smelled of lilac soap.

'You're okay, Tim.'

And then she walked away.

It was almost two on Saturday morning before Kevin arrived back. I was still awake when I heard the bike on the gravel at the side of the house. I went downstairs and turned on the yard light. Kevin was at the gate.

'Come in.'

'I'm going home.'

'You can go home in a while. Come in.'

He didn't move.

'Your bike is in the shed, you'll have to get it. You might as well come in.'

He walked back towards me, his face pale in the white light.

'Where did you go?'

'Out to Mullaghcreelan, that's all. I just stayed out there.'

We went into the kitchen and I made coffee. Kevin sat at the window, looking out into the night.

'I got him, didn't I?' he said quietly. 'It took a week but I got him. All the working together stuff, he thought I was coming round. I got him. I didn't have to scratch far to get him back to the way he is.'

'Fuck's sake, Kev, what's the point? What does that prove?'

'It proves that all his talk is nothing. He was at it the whole week. "Things could be this way, what way would you do it Kevin, do you think it's a good idea, will we move the cattle down the low farm?" All that shit, as though he could wipe out the last eighteen years. As if he had me now. It was as much as saying "School is over and that nonsense is finished, now I'll pull you in, stick your feet in the mud." But I knew what it was. He couldn't hide it too long. I knew I'd get him to show his true colours. And I did.'

'And you got your ribs kicked in as well. Did that cross your mind?'

'That's nothing.'

'It is something, Kev. What if he goes further the next time, what if you push him and he has a spade in his hand and he puts it through your head? Will that be nothing, too?'

'Let him try it.'

'And what? You get him first, you put a spade in his head? Cop on. This is the same as the stuff in Athy and the stuff in Carlow, it's the same thing. Cop on Kevin, before it's too late. You're nearly out of it. A few weeks and you're gone. What more do you want? A martyr's death?'

'I want him to admit what he is.'

'Come off it. You know, I know, Hannah knows, the whole place knows. Do you think he doesn't know? Draw the line. I don't want to lose you and Hannah doesn't want to lose you. And that's the way it's heading.' I hunkered down beside his chair.

'We're on the edge, Kev. The Shoebox Shitters are about to launch out into the big world. Please.'

He didn't look at me but he reached back and touched the side of my face with the side of his hand.

'Every time I'm with him, every time I see him at the head of a field, every time he drives the tractor into the yard, I want to stick in him, dig at him. But he carries on like everything is normal. And it isn't, never will be. I want to remind him. It's the only way I have of getting him to recognize that.'

'And how much can you take, how many times can you let him belt you round the place?'

'But I got him.'

'Yeah, yeah, you got him. It's done. You won, you won ages ago. He's lost you. Every time he tries to keep you, it's another time he's facing the fact that he's lost you.'

Kevin took his hand from my face and wrapped his arms around himself. He began to rock, gently, on his chair, still looking out through the window into the darkness. At first, I didn't realize he was crying but then the sobs came, hard and quiet, and the rocking went on, as if that could mask the sound of his pain.

I stood up and put my hands on his shoulders and let them move with the rhythm of his body.

'I might never be clear of him,' he said.

'You're nearly there.'

'I hope so.'

'Are your ribs all right?'

'Yeah, just a bit sore.'

'Maybe you should get them checked out.'

He shook his head.

'I'd know. They're all right.'

'Why don't you stay here tonight? Where's the point in cycling home? Stay here, I'll ring Hannah and tell her.'

'Maybe.'

I brought him upstairs and he lay down on my bed. Then I went to ring Hannah.

The phone rang for a long time before she answered.

'It's Tim, sorry for ringing so late.'

'It's okay,' her voice was deep and sleepy. 'Is he there?'

'Yeah, he's fine. He's going to stay.'

'Good. Thanks for ringing.'

'Okay, goodnight.'

I put the cups in the sink, locked the back door and put out the lights. When I got upstairs again, Kevin was asleep. I pulled the blankets over him and went back downstairs to sleep on the couch.

My father had gone shopping to Carlow and Kevin was still asleep when Hannah called on Saturday morning. I told her what had been said the night before.

'I think you're right,' she said. 'I think he'll be okay. Once he gets out of here, once he gets a new life going in Dublin, he'll get the worst of it out of his system.' She laughed.

'God knows, maybe he'll be back here farming some day. Content. Maybe we'll all be content in the end.'

'That's pushing things a bit,' I said. 'All of us happy ever after.'

'I didn't say happy, I said content. Settle for that, okay?'

'Okay.'

It was lunchtime before Kevin appeared. His eyes were rested, the paleness gone from his face.

'I did you out of your bed.'

'That all right. I wasn't stuck. What'll you eat?'

'Whatever.'

'Same as the rest of us then.'

'Grand.'

I took the makings of a salad from the fridge.

'How are the ribs?'

'Stiff, that's all. They're grand, no damage done.'

'Make yourself some tea.'

He made two mugs of tea and left one on the table beside me.

'Today we're going to do something,' I said. 'We're going to go somewhere, right? It's the weekend.'

'We could go to a dance in Athy.'

I looked at him, he was grinning. 'Feck off. We'll go to the pictures. Carlow. I'll ask my father for a loan of the car. Late show. And before that we'll go out to Mullagh-creelan or down the back river again. Something. We'll do something. We're on our holidays.' I was surprised at my own enthusiasm but it worked. Kevin's face lit up.

'You're on.'

He stood at the back door, looking across the yard to the sheds.

'Look at that heat. It must be near eighty.'

'Not far off it.'

'It's good to be alive.'

We sat at the kitchen table and ate.

'I'll go down home and get washed.'

'You can do that here, if you want.'

He shook his head. 'No. I want to go down. I'll have to some time, as well now as later. Anyway, the cattle need watering. And Hote.'

'I don't understand,' I said.

'If I don't water them they mightn't get watered all day. Would you like to be out in that heat without a drink?'

'No.'

'Well, that's what I want to do. Not for him. For them. He doesn't come into it.'

'Do you want a hand?'

Again, the shake of his head. 'No, I want to do it myself. I want to go down on my own.'

'Just take it easy, okay?'

'Yeah, I will. I'll be finished by three, I'll call up for you.'

'Hannah was here, this morning.'

'Right.'

We finished our meal. I put the dishes in the sink and watched Kevin cross the yard and take his bicycle from the shed. He waved as he rode away.

By the time I'd finished washing my father was back.

'I left a salad for you, in the fridge.'

'Thanks. Is Kevin gone?'

'Yeah. We're going off for a cycle later on, out to Kilkea, maybe go for a swim.'

'Grand.'

'I was thinking of clearing out the small shed, tidying up a bit, getting rid of the cardboard boxes and paper and stuff.'

'Great. It could do with a clean.'

I walked to the kitchen door.

'You want a loan of the car tonight?'

'What?'

'You wanted to borrow the car.'

'Ahm . . .'

'Why else would you be cleaning the shed on a day like this?'

I smiled.

'Only if you're not using it. We were thinking of going to the pictures in Carlow. We could thumb it.'

'Nah, I'll probably walk up for a pint. Just drive easy.'

'I will.'

I crossed the yard and opened the door on the small, musky shed that was filled with boxes and newspapers and odds and ends that would never be used again.

I hated that shed. In the winter it leaked and the wind lifted the edges of the corrugated iron roof, always threatening to launch it out into the orchard behind. On days like this, it was an oven.

I wished we could level it, open up the orchard so that it could be seen from the kitchen window but my father wouldn't hear of it. So I got on with it, piling the papers into the boxes and stacking them outside the door, sweeping the rubbish from the dry, clay floor, sorting out the paint tins and stacking them on the shelf above the door. I was happy doing that. And I was happy in the orchard, raking the huge bonfire that spewed flame into the dead heat.

I was happy.

*

Think of the trouble we took to avoid each other during your exams. Two years of good living and now it was almost done. Three weeks of examinations and you'd be free, we'd be free for each other.

I kept out of your way.

'It's better,' I said. 'Better to keep the exams clear of any distraction.'

So, for three weeks, I avoided the village when I thought you might be there. A couple of times you rang to tell me how you'd done in that day's paper but, otherwise, nothing.

I busied myself, knocking down the small shed. I worked methodically. Stripping the corrugated iron roof from it. Something I could have done eight months earlier, when my father died. It took me longer than I'd thought it would. The bolts were well buried in the timber and the sheets that I'd always imagined in flight on the back of a wind were almost impossible to dislodge. But, in the end, I managed it, levering the awkward, green roof off the wall and watching it rear up in the afternoon air, standing for a moment on the edge of the wall before clattering into the grass of the orchard headland.

I jumped down and set to work with a sledge, battering the metal into a manageable size, rolling it around the side of the shed and manhandling it into a trailer.

I didn't wait but drove it to the dump immediately and watched it tumble the thirty feet into the pit.

'I'm glad to be shut of that,' I said to the man at the gate. 'I've waited years to shift it.'

'You could've sold it for scrap.'

'I don't think so.'

Several times, that evening, I went upstairs and stood at my bedroom window and looked down on the open roof of the shed, in on the dark, dry floor and the walls that were suddenly, for only the second time in forty years, open to the air and the sky.

I'd told you what I wanted to do with the shed, knock it and open the orchard to the house.

That was in the weeks after my father died, early the previous November. You'd come up one Sunday to do some work on the English course. We stood under a low, grey sky and I talked about how much brighter the house would be with the shed levelled.

You walked around the yard, went into the sleeping orchard that was dreeping with fogged cobwebs, came back into the yard and stood at the kitchen door.

'I don't think that's going to work. It'll be too open when you come around the corner of the house.'

'Well, I'm not leaving that shed there. I hate it. We already have two other sheds and the garage.'

'Well don't knock it for a while,' you said.

And then, one afternoon, in January, as I was clearing my books in the classroom, you put your head around the door.

'Sir, can I have a word with you?'

There were three or four other students in the room.

I stepped into the corridor.

'Yeah?'

'I was thinking, about the shed – you know, the one you're going to knock down. I think you're right, about it blocking the light but I thought, if you knock it, why don't you use the stone to build a low wall across the orchard? It'll break up the empty space. That's all.' And you gave me one of your cheeky smiles, winked and were gone down the corridor, laughing to yourself.

The morning after I'd taken the roof off the shed I set about demolishing it.

I had a skip in the yard, to take the rubbish and the plaster and whatever wasn't reusable. I started work early, just after six, before the sun got hot, building a scaffolding of planks on barrels. I stripped to the waist and pulled on a pair of goggles and set about demolishing the front wall first, to leave myself a clear run to the skip with the barrows of rubbish from the other three walls.

It was hard work but, stone by stone, I sledged the wall down, cleaning the stones with a small hammer as I went and piling them in a corner of the yard.

Having waited so long to begin the work, I was pleased with how it was going, with my own patience in chipping away the old plaster from each rough stone and barrowing the debris away as soon as it was done, keeping the place as tidy as I could, not trying to do too much too fast. By late morning, when the sun was high and hot, I had worked halfway down the front wall. I left it at that and went inside to eat and rest. Sitting at the kitchen table, glancing across the white yard at the new landscape, the changing pattern of the disassembled stonework, I tried to *imagine how it would look by that night, when all the front wall would have gone. And how it would look the following day when the side walls came down and how the orchard would be, there in the space between the other sheds, when I had finished. And, finally, how the dry stone wall I'd build with the stones I'd taken down would look.*

By then your exams would be over. By then we'd be other people, so much would have changed between us. I sat and worried about that, about how easy it would be to adapt to what we expected of ourselves and of each other. We had been so diligent, there was always the possibility of our diligence being our destructions. What did we know of one another? Nothing really. It had all been a well-constructed game and we'd both stuck, rigidly, to the rules but we both knew that life isn't lived by rules, not if it's to be anything more than existence. These last two years had been just that, a form of existence and now we were facing real life, for better and worse. That afternoon, the wind changed. I went back outside and set to work on the side walls but the skies were piling black and stubborn over Mullarney and the wind was whipping along the lane and round the yard, curling little tornadoes of dust into the open shed, catching my breath each time the sledge crashed against the stonework.

And then the rain came. Huge drops that squatted on my skin for a second or two, to be followed by other drops, stabbing through the dark afternoon. I had just enough time to get myself inside before the skies opened and the yard was awash with a thunderous river of rain, rushing down the gullies, sweeping out into the lane and flooding the dykes.

That was last summer all over, wasn't it? Mornings of sunshine, afternoons of sudden rain, evenings when the skies dyed, slowly, back to blue again. How many of those afternoons was I caught out, cycling up Mullaghcreelan or on the straight between Grangenolvin and Kilkea, overtaken, without warning, by wind-lashed showers? Sheltering under the Round Bush or at gable end of Purcell's house. That was the kind of unreliable summer we had. But that was last year and this is now and the mornings, afternoons and evenings are one long blue sheet, pulled tight from end to end across the sky. As if that should be enough to keep us happy.

It was two days before I got back to the shed, two days before the skies cleared and the ground dried and the sun put in another appearance.

It was good to be back at work, eight days before you finished your exams, eight days to keep myself occupied, to get this work done. I wanted it finished by then, wanted the skip filled and gone, wanted the stones rebuilt into a wall across the top of the orchard. Almost as if I was preparing the place for a new bride, I thought. So much expectation. No point in thinking too much about it, get on with the work. And I did, I lost myself in the swinging sledge, in shovelling the dry plaster, barrowing it up the plank and into the crowded yellow skip, chipping back the stones and assessing how they might sit together. I worked through the day now, and on into the night and the side walls shrank to a few last stones in the clay floor.

And then there was just the back wall left. I got up early that Monday morning. Moved the scaffolding into place and began to knock it, swinging accurately, tipping the stones directly into the orchard grass. I was halfway down the wall when I noticed the square of mortar, camouflaged by years of dust but smoother than the stones around it. A square I'd never noticed in all my years of playing in the murky light of that shed.

There were figures scratched into the cement. Dipping my hand in a bucket of water, I wiped it clean. Figures scratched into the fresh cement with a nail.

22.8.1962

And there was more. I lifted the bucket and dashed the water against the remains of the wall. Below the figures were letters.

UMcH/JB

My parents' initials, scratched into the wet plaster nine days before their wedding day, almost thirty-three years earlier.

I sat on an upturned bucket, staring at the firm scratches from such a long time before. If I'd known, would I have levelled the shed? I wasn't sure. But I wanted you to see this. Now, where it was, before I removed any more of the stones.

I went inside and made a cup of coffee, waited until six

o'clock, until I knew you'd be home and then I rang. Do
you remember that?

    Your mother answered the phone and went to get you.

    Your voice, after so many days. 'Yes, hello.'

    'It's me.'

    'Are you all right?'

    'Yeah, I'm fine. How are the exams going?'

    'Okay, touch wood.'

    'Can I see you for an hour tonight? There's something I
found, something I wanted to show you.'

    'Of course. Where?'

    'It's up here. At the house.'

    'I'm just finishing my tea. I'll cycle up in half an hour.'

    'Are you sure? Do you want me to collect you?'

    'No. I'll cycle up. Honestly. See you about seven.'

    Such surprise on your face when you cycled into the
yard!

    'Wow, you haven't been wasting time, have you? It
looks great, you've got so much work done.'

    That smile, again.

    'I wasn't going to tell you till it was all done. I wanted
to have it done before you finished your exams but,
anyway, I found something I wanted to show you.'

    I led you across the yard, into the space that had been
the shed. We squatted beside the remaining wall and I
showed you the marks on the square of mortar and
explained them. You smiled, shyly. There were tears in
your eyes. You put your hand on mine.

    'You're not going to destroy this?'

'Hardly.'

'What are you going to do?'

'I'll take the piece out, cement it into the end of the wall when I build it across the orchard. The rest of it will be dry-stone but I'll cement this into one end. It'll still be the same thing, really. Won't it?' You nodded and touched the initials with your fingertips and then we stood up.

'Thirty-three years.'

And then you kissed me. First on the cheek but then your mouth was on my mouth and your tongue was on my tongue. The first time I tasted your taste in my mouth, there, with your back against the remains of the wall. You spread your arms wide along the wall and I held your head between my hands and we kissed for a long, long time.

'It's almost over,' I whispered.

You blinked and smiled.

'I'm glad you rang me.'

As soon as you'd gone, I set to work moving the block of plaster from the wall. I worked carefully but, in the end, it came away easily. My father had layered it on to a large, flat stone.

I put it in the garage and then went on with the rest of the work, finishing in darkness.

It rained the following day but that didn't stop me. I laid a line along the top of the orchard and began building the wall. It was back-breaking but I didn't stop. I worked through the day and the next, determined it would be *finished by the end of your exams. And it was. You rang from the school after the last exam.*

'Finished. All done.'

'How did it go?'

'At this second, I don't care, I'm just glad it's all over. And you?'

'Not doing much, you know.'

'Liar, you've been working, I bet.'

'A bit.'

'There's a few of us going up to the café, celebration, you know. We'd like if you'd come.'

'Now?'

'Yeah. Why not? Say goodbye to the class.'

'Okay,' I said. 'I'll meet you there in twenty minutes.'

It was a strange meal, more muted than I'd expected. I sat across the table from you, catching the light in your eyes, blue then green. You smiled a lot but you were quiet. I suppose you all were, seven teenagers on the edge of hope. As we left, we shook hands and hugged each other.

I thought of that on the day of your funeral as each of the six who were left came and hugged me outside the church. Fifteen months and a bitter lesson later. But on that afternoon we took our bikes from outside the café and walked down to the Square.

'So what are we doing?' I asked.

'I'm going home and I'm going to soak in a bath for at least five hours and tonight you're going to call for me and we're going for a drive somewhere and then we'll see.'

'That sounds good.'

'Maybe we'll drive down to Maganey Bridge and listen to the river again.'

You looked out at me, from under your fringe, your head to the side.

'I'll tell my parents you're coming over.'

I raised my eyebrows.

'I think they'll be happy. I know they'll be happy.'

*

'I got love bites all over me darlin',
love bites all over me tonight,
love bites all over me darlin',
the neighbours sayin' it ain't right.'

We were driving home from Carlow. Two o'clock in the morning. The windows open, warm air flowing over our faces. Kevin with his legs dangling out the window, singing, tunelessly, a song he was making up as he went:

'I got love bites on my neck,
darlin', darlin', hear me moan,
love bites on my chest and arms,
darlin', love bites on mah stones.'

He was warming to his subject.

'This could be a hit, this could make our fortune. Shooting up the US country charts. The Shoebox Shitters and their massive hit, "Love Bites", from the pen of Kevin Bracken.'

'D'you reckon?'

'I got love bites on mah fingers,
love bites on mah toes,
darlin', guess what I just found,
a love bite up mah nose.'

His laughter was a roar.

'That's it. All we need is a wrap-up verse and we're on our way. You can do the harmonies, okay?'

I shook my head.

'You're some guy.'

'Amn't I?'

I turned off the main road, down towards the Prumples-town Mill.

'What's this?' Kevin asked. 'Has my song gone to your head?'

I stopped the car on the margin near the bridge.

'You want to go swimming?'

I shook my head.

'What then?'

'I want to talk to you.'

'Sounds ominous.'

'No, it's not. I just want to talk to you. Two things.'

'Shoot.'

'First. Tonight was good crack, wasn't it? Going to the pictures, doing ordinary things. Having a laugh, taking the piss, but not getting into hassle. That kind of stuff?'

'Yeah.'

'Can we keep it that way? I know I said this before but I'm saying it again, Kev. You're my friend, all my life. I like it when you're a lunatic, you wake me up. But not the rest of it. And I want to say it now, tonight, when things are going well. Talk to me, talk to Hannah, don't just explode.'

'Okay. You're saying this for my own good, out of genuine and heartfelt concern for me.'

He slipped into the American twang of his song.

'Don't take the piss, Kev. I'm serious.'

'Okay, you're doing it because you love me, like a brother.'

I looked at him but there was no trace of irony in his face.

'Yes.'

'Okay. All right. And the second thing?'

'I want to talk to you, about what you said, about being gay, about what it means. It doesn't have to be now but it came up and then it dropped and I'm not sure how to bring it up again. But you wouldn't have mentioned it unless you wanted to talk. That's all. Like I said, it doesn't have to be tonight.'

He sat there, nodding.

'Sure. It's not the easiest thing to explain. I mean, it's more to do with feeling. I'll try, but not tonight.'

'Okay,' I said. 'Good.'

I started the car and reversed into a gateway and then drove back onto the main road.

'It doesn't have to be brotherly love, you know, us, if it works out some other way.'

'We'll see.'

We drove on in silence and then Kevin shouted, 'Got it, got it, got it. Last verse, sad verse.'

He closed his eyes and sang raucously, as we came down Barn Hill and into Castledermot:

> 'Love bites in the kitchen,
> love bites in mah bed,
> darlin', just for variation,
> why not give me a blow job instead.'

I drove slowly down the lane, past my house, and into Bracken's yard. There were two cars parked there.

'Hannah's still going out with your man?'

'Looks like it.'

I stopped the car. Kevin opened his door.

'Tea? Coffee?'

'No, I better get home, the car and all. You know how the old man gets a bit jumpy when I'm out late with it.'

'Okay. I'll see you after dinner.'

'Right.'

He beckoned towards the parked car.

'Do you think I should give this pair a verse of my song?'

'I don't know if they'd appreciate it.'

'Maybe not.'

'Okay then, goodnight.'

'Hey, thanks, brother.'

His mouth crooked into an embarrassed grin as he closed the door.

I swung the car around the yard, catching Hannah and her friend in the lights. She waved. And then the lights caught Kevin in the open kitchen door and he waved, too.

*

I remember the terror, driving up to your gate that night. What to expect, what was expected of me? And, worse, your father was in the garden, just inside the gate, stripped to the waist, cutting the box hedge that runs around the vegetable garden. A cigarette dangled from his lips. He looked up as the gate opened.

'Well, she can't be in trouble at school,' he laughed, the cigarette dancing as he spoke.

'No,' I said.

And then your mother was behind him, standing up from weeding the carrots.

'It's good to see you.'

'Thanks.'

'How are you?'

'Fine.'

'God rest your father, you must miss him.'

'I do,' I said.

'He was a lovely man.'

I smiled, not knowing what to say.

'You'll come in and have some tea.'

'Thanks but I just had it. Maybe later. I was looking for Jean.'

'She's inside. She's expecting you.'

'Right.'

I walked up the path and knocked on the open front door.

You were standing in the hall, laughing.

'Thanks very much for landing me in it.'

'You did very well.'

We walked back down the path.

'See you later,' you said.

'Enjoy yourselves.'

We sat into the car and your parents waved again.

'What did you tell them?'

'I didn't tell them anything. I said you were calling for me. That we were going out. That's all. It's not the first time, remember?'

'Yeah, I know, but this is different.'

'I hope so.'

'Where to?'

'Fraughan Hill. Let's go for a walk up Fraughan Hill.'

The evening was dry and cool. You were wearing jeans and a huge jumper that put the colours on the hill to shame.

'It's kind of strange, isn't it?' I said.

'Is it?'

'Well, after all this time.'

'Talk to me,' you said. 'Talk to me now. Tell me everything you feel. The good and the bad things, everything. Just tell me. Forget the school and all that stuff. Just talk to me, Tim.'

And I did. I talked about us, about the last two years, about my fantasies of you, about putting them out of my mind because they might drive me crazy. About the previous days, about wanting to get the wall finished. About my father's death. About my anxiety and dread and panic in the face of your expectations. It was a babble of doubt piled on doubt.

'I'm afraid,' I said.

'Afraid of what?'

'Of everything. Of what you expect of me and what I expect of you. Afraid that we waited for so long in the expectation of perfect happiness. Afraid of how it's all going to work out. Afraid, even, of going to bed with you. I've had so many fantasies about that, about what it's going to be like.'

'Mmmmm, tell me about them.'

'Come on, I'm serious.'

'So am I. I haven't been waiting with a virginal mind for two years either, you know. And, remember, I was the one who started all this. Do you think I curled up in bed every night and never thought about what it might be like to be with you?'

'But it may not happen the way either of us imagined.'

'Are you frightened of what we want or are you frightened of being tied to me? Is this about travelling hopefully? Are you shit-scared now that you've arrived, because if you are, say so. Just say it.'

'No.'

'It's possible. I know that. I know what the last two years is hanging on, one dance and a couple of conversations. I know that as well as you do. And, after all that,

there might be nothing to it, I know that too. I'm not thick.'

Your voice was very serious, deeper than before. You'd stopped climbing and your hand was on my arm. I was standing slightly above you, facing down across the valley. You were looking up into my face, your eyes intense, green now, no sign of the blue that came and went. And your hand light on my sleeve. You looked so young and, yet, so solemn. So beautiful. I knew, while you were talking, how much I loved you and how strong you were, how happy our lives could be in spite of anything. 'Come clean, all right? And I'll do the same. Maybe I'm living in a dream, maybe I don't see all the problems you see. But I'm afraid, too, about lots of things. About what you expect of me, about being with you all the time, about how we'll deal with things when they go wrong, about being away from you when I go to college. About going to bed with you. I've never slept with anyone. The furthest I've got is messing around with guys after dances, and that's two years ago. I've even missed out on whatever I might have learned in the meantime. So, I'm shit scared, too. We both are. But we could stay that way for ever.'

You took your hand away. 'If it's just fear that's okay. If it's something else, if you feel I'm reeling you in, say it.'

'I don't feel that, at all. I feel happy, more than happy. Ecstatic. But I know things have a habit of going wrong.'

'So?'

'Sometimes, when we put too much store by things, they go wrong. I've seen it happen.'

'Tell me about it.'

'I will, some time, but not now. Not here, not starting out. I'm not going to let it get in the way.'

'Good.'

You had a way of saying that one word, a short, sharp way that was totally reassuring.

We walked on up Fraughan Hill, hand in hand, up to the timberline and, then, we sat on the grass looking down across the countryside, picking out the landmarks in the Barrow Valley. The sugar factory in Carlow; Minch Norton's in Athy; the Moat of Ardscull; the round tower in Castledermot; the power-station chimney in Portarlington.

'I wished,' you said, quietly, 'when your father died, I wished I could come and be with you. I thought of you all that time. The night after he died, I lay in bed at home and I wanted to get up and go to you.'

'You came to the funeral.'

'The whole school went to that. That was nothing. I wanted to go up and stay with you. I thought of you in the house and your father laid out and all your relations and stuff and I knew that'd be all right. But I knew there'd be the night after he was buried and the nights after that, when you'd be alone. I wished I could go to you. Just to be there. Not to do anything. I didn't think of it that way. Just to sleep with you. For comfort.'

I put my arm around you, pulled you close to me, buried my face in the pleated wool of your jumper, smelled the smell of your clothes and, deeper still, of your skin. I was so much in love with you. So lost without you.

*

Kevin and I cycled out to Mullaghcreelan the following afternoon. We left our bikes in the carpark.

'Do you reckon they're safe? There's a lot of dodgy people around here on a Sunday, into the car and off with them.'

'Safe as houses,' Kevin said. 'I don't think there's anyone here who's going to dare mix it with the Shoebox Shitters. The very name strikes fear into their bourgeois bowels.'

'I'll remind you of that if the bikes are gone when we come back.'

'Trust me, compadre, you need to learn the meaning of trust.'

Kevin was in his cowboy drawl again.

We crossed the carpark, packed with picnickers, and went up through the evergreens. The woods were swarming, children screaming in the trees, dogs chasing through the undergrowth, adults climbing stiffly towards the summit.

We cut around the hill to avoid them, past the sandpit and down through a half-hidden valley that we called the tropical forest, and then out on to the low path, at the back of the wood. The only trace left of the crowds was the occasional voice from the top of the hill. Few had the energy or the enthusiasm to go down the other side of

Mullaghcreelan. Even in early summer, when that part of the hill was flooded with bluebells, few Sunday afternooners made the effort to get there. It was left to Kevin and me, just as it was that afternoon.

We stretched out on the grassy bank and let the sunlight filter through the leaves and wash us. And while we lay there, eyes closed, Kevin talked and talked. About wanting to prove himself and trying to find out what he needed and where it could be found.

'You never said anything to me, when you started going through this,' I said.

'What could I say? I didn't know what to say to myself, I didn't know what I was thinking, any of that stuff. I'm not even sure I do now, it's only the start.'

'But you're sure you're gay?'

'I think I'm sure,' he said laughing. 'I know that sounds thick. It's like me asking you, are you sure you're straight?'

He sat up. His face had this incredibly earnest look.

'It's like the way we always talked about girls, about sex, about wanting to find out, half bullshit, half-wishing it would happen. Like when I was dancing with that girl in Carlow there was this feeling, wanting to know what it would be like to do it with her but really, a lot of the time, I think about what it's like to kiss a guy, to touch a guy, to be touched. If that girl had gone outside with me, I'd have gone, to find out. But it's not what I really want.'

He looked at me.

'That probably doesn't make any sense to you.'

'It does a bit.'

'Does it?'

'I know about the wanting to find out thing. I'd go with any girl if I thought she'd do stuff because I want to know what it's like. I'd rather find out and make mistakes with someone like that, at a dance, someone I'd never see again, and not make a complete gobshite of myself with someone I really wanted to go with. It's about sex, not love.'

'Some of it is,' Kevin said. 'But some of it isn't. Some of it's about feeling a certain way and that's the bit I can't really explain. Just like you probably couldn't explain to me why you like one girl more than another, what the real difference is, beyond the way she looks or what she wears. If it was just sex, just biology, I could be satisfied by doing it myself, so could you. It's the other person, the connection, what that sets up inside, that's the bit I can't explain.'

I lay in the sun watching Kevin. He was rocking slowly, speaking deliberately, his hands clasped around his knees, looking away from us, through the trees. The light was catching his eyes and he looked so certain about what he was saying. So much more certain than I was about anything.

'I never thought that much about it,' I said. 'Beyond shifting someone at the school dances or watching some of the girls down the town. It was all in my head. I never really did much about it, the chance never seemed to come. I never met anyone who was dying for me to sweep her off her feet. Or anything else.'

'So what do you want to do?'

'What do you mean?'

'Just that.'

'I don't know. Keep looking, I suppose. I'm just waiting for someone who'll make the first move, I think, just waiting.'

'That's what I'm doing, too. First I find out what it's like. I have no idea, same as you have no idea, what it's like to kiss someone, to touch them, to take off their clothes or have them open your shirt and run their hands down your belly. I have the same dream as you have. It's the same dream, you know.'

'It's a nice dream.'

'And it won't always be just that.'

I took a deep breath and closed my eyes.

'Does it make you horny, talking like this? With me.'

And then I opened them again. Kevin was still staring away through the trees.

'Maybe.'

'What does maybe mean?'

'It means I didn't think about it that way. I was just talking, same way you were talking last night. The rest of it is a different step, it's a next step and I haven't thought too much about that. I've made sure not to. It was never a question between us and it doesn't have to be. But it could be.'

He shrugged. 'That's kind of up to you.'

'And you.'

'That's okay.'

'And what'll it be like?' I asked.

'Divine intoxication.'

'What are you talking about?'

'Emily Dickinson.'

'I remember you telling Rusty, in English class, that you didn't like her.'

'And I didn't but I do now.'

'The thing is, see, Kev, I don't know what I feel. I mean, I feel relaxed with you, I know you all my life. It might be fine. I'm curious about what it might be like, what you said about what it's like to have someone else touching you. I'm curious. But what if it doesn't work out?'

'Then it doesn't. It's something we tried. We didn't stop being friends when I got on the school football team and you didn't.'

'And that's it?'

'Maybe it is. It might be as simple as that. I don't know, I know nothing more about how we'll feel than you do. I'm not pushing you, you know that.'

'I do.'

'I don't have all the answers, I'm being honest with you. I'm just trying to find my own way, you know.'

'Jesus, this is a great flood of honesty on all sides.'

We lay back in the sun and listened to the birds and the trees cricking in the afternoon heat. Now and then a voice dripped down from the top of the hill but, mostly, there was just the heat and the great stillness of the trees above us and, then, the sound of Kevin's breathing. I looked across at his sleeping head, the tanned skin and the sun-bleached, curly hair.

I felt so much for him. Pity, admiration, desire. I leaned

across and kissed his mouth, the strangeness of kissing that mouth, how one kiss could change the way I thought of Kevin, of how I thought of his face. How different it felt from the way I might have imagined it. Sight and touch and no comparison.

He didn't open his eyes but he raised his left hand and cupped it round the back of my head so that my face was against his hair. I worked my hand under his shirt, pushing it up until his belly was uncovered, fanning my fingers across his chest. He lifted my head away from his and kissed me, his lips dry against mine. And then his tongue was in my mouth and he had pulled me onto him, his hands excited in my hair. Our kisses were deep, our bodies locked into each other, deeper and deeper until we could no longer breathe and I rolled away and we lay, again, side by side.

'It wasn't the worst thing ever, was it?' Kevin said quietly.

'No, not for the first time.'

'The going of an island soul to sea.'

'More Emily Dickinson.'

'Not more, just the same.'

'So you do like her, you're not a real queer. You hanker after Emily Dickinson.'

'The dead Emily Dickinson.'

'You're a necrophiliac.'

'I'm a bisexual necrophiliac.'

'And what am I?'

'You are,' he hesitated. 'You are someone I'm going to fuck, someone who's going to fuck me.'

Next morning, cycling to work, I thought about what we'd done on Mullaghcreelan. In the light of morning, what did I feel? Excited, tense, anxious for the next time but not sure why. Was it just like when we were kids, when we took off our clothes and ran up and down Rice's Hill, just for the thrill of it, just because we knew our parents would be disgusted?

Maybe it was no more than that. But, then, so what?

I didn't suddenly feel I never wanted to see Kevin again, I didn't feel embarrassed, I didn't feel anything at all, other than curiosity.

The only thing I wished was that our next meeting was over and done with. What if Kevin regretted what he'd said and what we'd done? What if he felt he'd opened up to me and shouldn't have? What if he was the one to be filled with regret after all? That was my only doubt but I cycled faster, letting the wind tear everything from my head except the thrill of speed and, as the bike breasted a hill, I gave myself up to the pleasure of spinning through the new morning.

*

I finished the wall the following week. The first dry stone wall I'd ever built. I was as proud as hell. You stood in the orchard, looking down the meandering stones from end to end of the headland, smiling wryly.

'I like the way it's not a straight line,' you said.

'It wasn't meant to be a straight line, I built it that way. You don't like straight lines.'

'Oh, you made it crooked it for me? To please me,' you said sarcastically.

'Yes, I did.'

You kissed me and we walked the length of the wall.

'See,' I said.

I pointed to the stone my parents had scratched their initials and date into. It was cemented into the end of the wall, away from the brunt of wind and rain that came up the orchard in the autumn and winter.

'I like that. You did it really well. I think they'd be happy with that.'

'Do you?'

'Yeah, I think that's good. It's the place for it.'

'We walked back to the other end of the wall. I took a bucket of damp cement from behind the stones and spread a layer of it on to a large flat stone at the base of the wall.

'Now it's our turn.'

Your face lit up and then I saw a tear and, then, another.

'If you want to,' I said. 'Maybe it's not the time.'

'Oh, it is.'

I handed you a rusted, flat-headed nail.

'I found that in the shed. It seemed appropriate.'

You knelt in the damp grass and scratched your initials. I took the nail from you and scratched mine beside them. 'Now, the date,' I said.

You finished the work and we stood back to look at it.

JD/TB

30.6.1994

You reached back and took my hand. The sun shafted up the orchard, polishing the small hard fruit on the trees. I've tried often, in the past weeks, to reach back to that afternoon but I never get beyond a point of observation. I can never get inside. I watch you and me there, as though I was looking at a film, but I have no sense of being part of the scene. I know there was an intensity then, a mysticism about that afternoon, but it's beyond me. I see it but I cannot sense it. I know what you said and what I said but I cannot hear the voices. Our mouths are moving, your tears are falling, you're taking my hand, we're standing there but this is all. I cannot get inside the scene anymore, as I cannot get inside you.

Sometimes that frightens me, not just that the dreams of you haven't come but that I have lost my saviour and next I may lose my faith, that my creed may slip away. I recite it over and over, remind myself with your photographs, with the bits and pieces, the paraphernalia of what must pass for our lives together. I open your perfume bottles sparingly, for fear your memory will evaporate with the scent inside. I spread your photographs out across the kitchen table, I leave them there overnight, as if you *might put yourself together again, in the hot twilight of these summer hours. I listen for your step on the stair, the creak of the board at the turn, the soft sound of your bare foot, the same sound I heard so often and never considered not hearing again. You, in your striped blue nightshirt, at the open window, leaning out over the still garden, tasting the apple and damson of the night. Or. You at the mirror brushing the chestnuts through your hair, a trace of lilac when you slipped out of your dress.*

How can I live without you, in a house that's haunted by your presence? I turn over in the night, the window is open at the head of my bed and I think of my father and how he turned his face to the wall, the bed so big, his body so insignificant, so frail. I become aware of the wall to my face and the emptiness of my own bed. And I want you to come back to me. I scatter some of your powder on the pillow and bury my face in it. I want to suffocate in you but there is only absence. I want to fuck your absent body because longing wells up in me like anger. I drive myself against the memory of you until I have come on the crumpled sheet and fall asleep, exhausted, terrified by the loss of you. And when I wake, as soon as light lifts its head in the fields outside, I imagine you there. The scent from the pillow, the heat, the dampness where we might have fucked. It all says you. But the garden is empty, the night haze lifting to show me the trees laden with fruit, the wall straggling across the headland, the yard empty. And the creak of the stairboard under my own foot

reminds me that you didn't come up the stairs, singing
softly in the night.

The photographs are still jigsawed across the table. I
imagine one or two have been moved, the ones you pre-
ferred brought to the top, to remind me. I stand, naked, in
the kitchen. The sun is aching over me. The thought that
you might have been here, that you might silently have
rearranged the pictures in the night, might have come so
close and could not come any closer, breaks my heart.
There is no loneliness like this, nothing worse than the
beauty of the day and the beauty of your face and the
desolation that I feel.

I am desolate without you. I will sit up all night in the
kitchen and wait for you.

And I do. I sit with the windows open and wait all
night but you don't come. I think I see your shadow in the
garden. I go outside and sit in the hammock that drifts
between the trees. I search the branches for some sign of
your passing. I walk up and down between the trees,
ducking the heavy fruit, imagining, wanting.

I lie down again in the hammock and come on to the
damp grass, because nothing else can bring me sleep, and
wake with the first slice of sunlight. What else is there for
me to do?

*

'You're on a wedding next Saturday,' the headwaiter said.
I was just about to leave the restaurant. 'Sorry about that,

says bollocky Bill the sailor-oh. I'll need you here for set-up at half-eleven. You'll be out by seven. You can take Monday off instead, all right?'

'Yeah.'

'Catering is a way of life, not just a career, says bollocky Bill. And you're just passing through. Aren't you lucky! Right, off you go.'

I cycled home slowly. The house was empty. Upstairs I ran a bath. My clothes were soaked with sweat. I threw them into the washing machine and went and lay in the tepid water and listened to the birds in the garden outside. A tractor passed along the lane. I wondered if Kevin was driving it. I wondered what it would be like to have him come in here. I imagined him on the stairs, pushing the half-open door wide and coming into the bathroom, cupping the water in his hands and pouring it over my head. I smiled at the thought. I had a vision of Kevin as John the Baptist, he'd look the part, anointing the people in the desert, cupping the water and baptising them, letting it run through his fingers and roll in beads through their hair and down their shoulders. And then I imagined him dipping his hands below the surface of my bath water, touching my calf, bending over the bath and kissing my wet face. I wanted him to do that, I wanted to move on from the place we'd been. I wanted to know more.

'Why don't we go for a walk down Mullarney?' I said. We were standing in Bracken's yard that evening.

'We're off.'

We cut across the Square, down the Green and over the bridge.

'What'll we do the weekend? Do you fancy going up to Dublin for the day on Saturday?'

'I can't,' I said. 'I'm caught for work that day, a wedding.'

'I might go up, just to get away from here. Might stay in my aunt's house. I'll suss it out, she wants me to go into digs with her. Maybe the two of us could go up another weekend.'

'That'd be good.'

We crossed the fields and another bridge, coming out among the ruined farm buildings at Mullarncy.

'This was great cowboy country, when we were kids.'

I nodded.

'Some of the fiercest gunfights of our time were held in this here street, remember? The sun coming down into the eyes of the Cisco Kid, the odds against him, a gun barrel in every window, death staring him in the face, but he never flinched and he never doubted the talent of his own gun, blazing away without ever having to reload, killing three men with one calculated ricochet. And he emerged at the other end with just one flesh wound to his arm. Do you remember those fights?'

'I was those men,' I said. 'I remember you tried to persuade me to fall out the top window once.'

'I did not.'

'Yes you did, you put three empty sacks on the ground there and told me I'd be all right.'

'And did you do it?'

'Would I be here now if I did? It's twenty feet.'

'I don't remember that, at all,' Kevin laughed.

'Well, I do. I was standing up there and you were here and I remember thinking how far down it was and then you spread out the sacks. You said that was what they used in the pictures.'

'And so it is.'

'Thanks.'

We sat on the low wall outside the ruined farmhouse. The sun was an orange just above the village. There were long, deeply burned shadows on the ground. No breeze, no birdsong, not a breath of air, no sound from where the rooftops shone under its light. No other world but ours. I told Kevin about what I'd thought as I lay in the bath that afternoon.

'I wish I was telepathic,' he said, turning to face me, his mouth inches from mine.

'Let's go inside. In case.'

We walked into the ruined house, its walls scarred with decades of initials and dates and graffiti, up the rotting stairs. It was hot and shaded in the upstairs room. Kevin stopped immediately inside the door, and pulled me towards him, leaning back against the rough wall and we kissed. Our mouths were locked, my body hard against his, his hand fumbling for my jeans, neither of us able to breathe properly, and then my hands were wrestling his belt and we slid, together, to the ground, his hand on my prick and mine finding his, our tongues still working furiously, afraid to move apart, eyes closed, afraid to look

at what we were doing, afraid of what we'd lose or find,
the surge of my come across his hand, his cock jerking
against my palm, jerking, jerking, till he came too and still
we went on kissing, our bodies, belly to belly, sliding in
the wet hotness until, at last, exhausted, we slid apart and
lay on our backs.

I saw the white glint on Kevin's belly. I looked at him,
his eyes were closed and I thought, for a moment, he was
asleep but then he spoke. His lips were dry, the words lost.
Licking his lips, he began again.

'Bred as we, among the mountains, can the sailor
understand? The divine intoxication of the first league out
from land. E. Dickinson, author.'

I smiled to myself. Kevin's eyes were still closed. He
leaned across and rubbed his palm on my wet belly.

'This was our first league out from land. And it was
okay, wasn't it?'

'Yes,' I said. 'It was.'

*

*There's one box full of your photographs and one box with
your letters. The letters that came last year, when you
were away at college, and the notes you left for me, about
the house. Two or three lines on sheets of paper, messages
that would mean nothing to anyone else, your cryptic
reminders of what we'd done or what we meant to do.
Twenty-word love songs, you were good at that. I remember a conversation we had, the week before you left for
Dublin, sitting in the kitchen, looking out at the torrents*

of rain that swept away the ends of that excuse for summer. I was feeling miserable, back at school, and you were about to go away.

'It's only Monday to Friday,' you said. 'I'll be home the weekend. And you did say you'd be coming to Dublin on Wednesdays.'

'I know.'

'So, why so down?'

'Don't know.'

'Bullshit.'

'I don't.'

'Listen, Tim, I haven't spent the last five years stalking you just to let you fob me off with that. Speak.'

'Just that it's been such a good time, this summer. You and me.'

'And the weather.'

As you spoke, a sheet of rain slapped the kitchen window. I smiled.

'Not much of a smile,' you said.

'Just that it might all capsize, when you're gone. Hard to keep it going when you're in college. Things change, people change, and don't tell me that's not true.'

'I know they do.'

Your face was, suddenly, serious.

'But someone might come into your life, some new teacher, some new woman in town, someone you meet.'

'Don't take the piss,' I said. 'That's not going to happen but things will be different. It was all so close, so confined in school. It was unnatural. It'll be different now, you'll

100

be out there. Lots of people, new situation. It's a new world. I know. I've been there.'

'So what do you want me to do, not go to college?'

'Jesus, no, course not. That'd be a recipe for disaster. It's just being back at school and all that. I'm always this way in the autumn.'

'You know, you never told me about college. About what you did there, who your friends were. That stuff. Never a word.'

I shrugged. 'It was nothing much. Football, study, films, music. The usual.'

'No women?'

'A few.'

'Did you sleep with them?'

'One or two.'

'Tell me about them.'

'No,' I laughed.

'Go on, tell me.'

'No. There's nothing to tell.'

'Go on.'

'You tell me about your experiences,' I said.

'Okay. Derry Rogers, after a youth club barbecue. Light petting. I was fourteen. I was thinking about making my move on you. Tommy Byrne, after a school dance. Attempted heavy petting, nothing happened. I thought, what the hell am I doing with him, I don't even like him. Made my excuses and left. I was fifteen. A few dances, a few smooches. Then you. The long wait. This summer. The future. Dah dah!'

A fanfare and a little dance around the table and you were sitting on my lap.

'Now you tell me.'

'Honestly, there's nothing to tell.'

'Do you know something?' you said.

'What?'

'We never talk about the past. You've never told me about who your friends were when you were growing up. None of that. If you died tonight I wouldn't have a clue who to tell.'

'My aunt,' I said.

'No, I'm serious. You never tell me about you and you never ask me anything about me, about growing up, any of that stuff.'

'That's because I'm jealous, of your past.'

'Be my guest. You are my past.'

'Well I'm jealous of your future, then. Of what might happen. It worries me.'

'And you think I don't worry at all? Do you know why I want to do this degree?'

'Yeah, to get a job.'

'Yes, to get a job, so I can do what I want to do, so I can be my own boss, so I can get my own van, so I can say I'm a qualified horticulturalist and no job is beyond me. And why do I want all this, apart from loving gardens? Because I want to know that at the end of my three years in college I won't have to try to get a job somewhere at the other end of the country from you, that I can be sure I have a career that can start here and* continue here, because I want to be with you, because I want to live with you.'

'You just want to get your hands on my acre of garden.'

'Actually,' you said, 'I just want to get your hands on me.'

Later that night, when I was driving you home, you asked me, again, about the past.

'Tell me about the first woman you slept with.'

'Why?'

'I want to know.'

'She was just someone I met.'

'In college?'

'Yeah,' I lied.

'Was she beautiful?'

'Yes, she was.'

'And what happened?'

'I don't know,' I said. 'We kind of lost each other along the way. Nobody's fault, I think. It was always going to be that way.'

'Did you love her?'

'Yes, I did.'

'And did she love you?'

'I think she did. Afterwards she said she didn't but I think she did.'

You didn't push me any further and I was grateful.

When I got back home, there was a note on my pillow.

> I couldn't live without you,
> I only live to come back to you,
> I love you, Jean

It's there with the other notes and letters, there in the tin box on my desk.

Oh, and I meant to tell you about Kevin and Hannah but the time never seemed right and, like you said, we never seemed to talk too much about the past. And that's why I'm telling you the whole story now, because I know it's not too late.

*

The wedding was worse than I expected. Busier than the tour buses, louder than the Americans, a huge room full of people determined to get as drunk as possible, as quickly as possible. Or so it seemed to me. Even the headwaiter was impressed by their loudness and arrogance. 'Look at that, amazing, a hundred and twenty hyenas on their hind legs and all in one room. Quite amazing. Bollocky Bill has never seen the like of this before.'

We were standing, the headwaiter and the ten waiters and waitresses, at the top of the restaurant, waiting for the wedding guests to finish their soup.

He threw his eye over the crowd. 'Three-ring circus,' he muttered. 'And I'm expected to be the ringmaster. Jesus wept, look at the mouth on the groom's father, it's a wonder the young fellow survived to see this day. That man could eat a farmer's arse through a cane-bottomed chair. Someone give me a whip before I wade in to serve the main course. All right, folks, mind your hands and do not, I repeat, do not get within snapping distance of the groom's father. He's rabid.'

He smiled sweetly and called to the end of the line. 'All right, clear the soup please. Thank you.'

By mid-afternoon the windows of the restaurant were all thrown open but, still, the room was a cauldron. Which helped. It made people uneasy, anxious to be out of it, eager to take their drinks out on to the lawn. The place was cleared by half past five and we were out of it by half past six.

'You survived,' the headwaiter said as I walked down the back stairs. He was sitting just inside the door, smoking.

'I did.'

'And now you're free. Free to pursue the young ones for forty-eight hours. Aren't you the lucky sod. When I was your age I was eighteen.'

He laughed at his own joke. 'I envy you. Be young, stay young, ride everything in sight, says bollocky Bill. It's gone soon enough and it doesn't ever come back. Ever. Now, go in peace.' He waved me away.

I cycled down the drive from the hotel. The wedding guests were sitting in groups under the umbrellas on the lawn. Nearer the gate, the air smelled of trees. Elder, chestnut, lime. I turned on to the road for Castledermot. It was a gorgeous evening. And I was happy. I had money in my pocket and two free days ahead of me. And, in a way, I was glad that Kevin was in Dublin. After the intensity of that evening in Mullarney I was happy to be alone. Not that I regretted what we'd done, I was looking forward to what might happen next, but I'd always been glad of the times when Kevin and I were thrown apart.

Our lives had been so intertwined since childhood that I sometimes needed freedom like this. So I savoured that evening and the prospect of Sunday, lazing around the house, making dinner with my father, maybe driving down to Tullamore to see my aunt.

My father was just leaving the house when I got home. 'Your dinner's on the cooker. I'm going up to collect Mrs Herron. Tommy is in hospital in Naas, I told her I'd run her up.'

'What happened to him?'

'Slipped off a ladder, painting the house. Did his back in. He'll be all right but she's anxious to see him.'

'Okay. I'll see you later. I might go out but I won't be late.'

'How was the wedding?'

'I'm just glad I wasn't invited.'

He laughed. 'You get them like that.'

I went inside, ate my dinner, read the paper, thought about swimming but decided on a walk instead. I went down the river, through the Cavalry Field, across Joe Shea's bridge and into the Rocks. The river was barely moving, low and slow over the smooth stones. It dozed at the roots of the yellow flags before struggling away again, racing a little where it deepened and then falling again to a trickle. Ahead of me, two hundred yards down the bank, a couple walked arm in arm. They were going away from me, leaving the river and moving through the furze bushes, making for the back of Rice's Hill. As they turned, I recognized Hannah. And then the guy she was with, the

one who'd driven us home from Athy. On an impulse I
followed them, keeping my distance, ambling as though by
chance, ready to show surprise if they turned back and
met me. But they showed no signs of that. Their heads
were bent together, now and then he put his arm around
Hannah's shoulders and pulled her towards him, a couple
of times they stopped to kiss. And then they went through
the gap in the ditch and on to the hill. I followed, keeping
clear of the dry twigs and fallen branches under the ditch,
stepping through the rich, heavy furze. Instinctively, I
knew where they were going. To the little hollow where
we'd played soldiers as kids. It was a clear patch of grass,
sunk between rocks and furze bushes.

I worked my way round until I came to the edge of the
hollow from the other side, squatting between two rocks,
peering through the sharp yellow flowers, down into the
floor of the hollow. And there they were. Hannah lying in
the grass, her dress unbuttoned, opened about her, like
bright butterfly wings. And he, I didn't even know his
name, was kneeling above her, his face buried in her
shoulder. I tried to cut him out of the picture. I wanted
this to be just Hannah, with me watching her. I leaned
forward for a clearer view. Her eyes were open but she
was looking away from him. I was excited by her, by her
body, by her open dress, by the way her brown legs jutted
out from under his body, by the way her eyes stayed open
all the time, searching the sky and the furze bushes,
unconcerned with what was going on. I felt strangely
elated that this guy, whom I despised without knowing,

was making no impression on Hannah. I didn't want him to. And, I realized, it had little to do with him and a lot to do with me, with an unexpected possessiveness I felt for her, a desire that I had never suspected. Not that I'd ever do anything about it. I knew Hannah too well. I'd never had a sexual thought about her in my life. She was just Kevin's sister and that was that. But seeing her here, even the fact of following her, had changed something. Just as talking to her, the week before, had changed something else.

And so I stayed there, watching her with this guy. He kissed her neck and the side of her face but she didn't respond and, in the end, he rolled away and straightened his clothes. But Hannah still lay there, her dress open, the sun on her belly, her eyes lazing on the furze bushes. On me? For a moment I thought so but I was well hidden. Still, I backed away, just in case, ducking through the bushes, heading back to the river, keeping in the shelter of the hedge until I was into the Rocks and clear of the hill.

I walked fast and I kept walking, till I came out at the bridge at Halfmiletown and then I started back along the Barrack road, heading for home.

What did I feel? Guilt? Not then. Satisfaction? Yes, but not because I'd seen something I wasn't meant to, not because I'd seen an almost naked girl. I found it difficult to understand what I felt. Whatever satisfaction there was hinged on the fact that this, clearly, was the end of a relationship, the frustrated in pursuit of the disinterested. But that, too, was confusing. I had no reason, beyond a loose friendship with Hannah, to care one way or the other about what happened in her love life, so what was the source of my satisfaction? From our brief conversation on the lane, from the things I'd never known about her, from finding out that she was as clever as Kevin or me, from her flirtation with her younger brother's friend? Could be; could be any or all of these.

It was almost dark by the time I got home. My father was back from Naas.

'How's the patient?'

'All right. Gave himself a right whack. He'll be in for a while. He's very fed up, delighted to see us. I might run up again tomorrow.'

'Tell him I was asking for him.'

We sat in the kitchen, half-watching something on TV. It was almost twelve when the phone rang.

'I hope that's not bad news,' my father said, as he went to answer it.

I turned down the sound on the TV.

'It's for you,' he said.

'Who is it? Kevin?'

'No, it's Hannah.'

I went into the hall and picked up the phone.

'Did I get you out of bed?'

'No.' I said. 'We were just watching telly. Is everything okay?'

'Yeah.'

'I thought it might be Kev.'

'Well now you know. Listen, are you working tomorrow?'

'Nope. I was on a wedding today. I'm off till Tuesday.'

'And have you anything planned?'

'Not a thing.'

'Do you fancy going for a cycle? I'm at a loose end myself but if you've anything else doing just say so.'

'No, honestly. That'd be great.'

'I'll give you a shout then, about two.'

'Good. I'll go out and put new tyres on the bike.'

'Piss off.'

*

I still have visions of you, the first time I visited you in Dublin, the Wednesday afternoon of your first week in college. For once, that autumn, it wasn't raining. Instead it was a balmy October afternoon. I parked in Stephen's Green and walked down to the Grafton Street gate and waited. And then I saw you, coming through the crowds, hurrying along the path in the Green, the leaves lifting behind your boots.

Your hair the colour of those leaves. You were wearing black jeans and a white shirt and your jacket was open. I saw how young and bright and beautiful you were. I played a game, telling myself you were a woman hurrying to meet someone else. You would pass by in a moment and I'd be filled with envy for whoever it was you were going to. I remember that moment vividly. The pleasure of denial that wasn't real, the postponement of delight for just an instant, the vision of you hurrying along the path, weaving through the crowds until you saw me. And how

your face lit up, the earnestness gone, delight in your eyes.
I was so happy, so fortunate to have you. It was a moment
of realization that what had been promised in our lives
would be delivered.

*

We cycled through Woodlands, out the Levitstown road,
across to Kilkea, over the Big Bog, on to Hobartstown and
up into the hills behind Bolton. The afternoon was hot and
empty, the roads deserted. We stopped every few miles to
rest on the roadside banks.

We talked about Kevin and Bracken and work and
weather and holidays.

'I can't wait for them,' Hannah said. 'I'll be away like a
shot, last two weeks of July.'

'Where are you going?'

'Spain. It won't be that much hotter than here but it'll
be a change.'

'Who's going with you?'

'Three of the girls from the factory. We went last year
as well, remember?'

I shook my head.

'How flattering. Come on, let's go.' She stood up, in
mock anger. 'I'm not sitting around here with someone
who doesn't know whether I'm at home or away. Get your
ass in the saddle.'

We freewheeled down the back road from Bolton, into
Moone, crossing the main road and turning back towards
Kilkea.

'If I'd known we were going this far I'd have eaten two dinners,' I said.

'I sit in the factory all week dreaming about this. It's okay for you, you get out every day. I get up, get on the bus, go to work, come home on the bus and it's night again. This is freedom. I'm making the best of it.'

'Thanks for the philosophy.'

'We'll stop at the High Cross, I'll buy you a drink.'

'Done.'

We sat outside the pub and drank slowly. A couple of children played in the yard, their parents sitting quietly at a table under the trees.

'Wouldn't it be great to have that millionaire now?' Hannah said. 'Not to have to worry about work tomorrow.'

'I don't,' I said. 'I'm off.'

She poured some of her drink over me.

'Shut up, smart arse, I'm daydreaming.'

She closed her eyes.

'Do you think Kevin's going to get it together?'

I looked at her. 'I hope so.'

'But what do you think?'

'I think he will.'

'He had bad times, I know. I never got hit. For some reason, he never dodged the bad times. He could have, often.'

'I know that.'

'He just came at them, head on.'

'That's the way he deals with it. I wouldn't, but that's his way.'

'And you think he'll be okay?'

'Yes, I do.'

'I don't think he'll ever forgive my father, though, do you?'

'No.'

'Still, as long as he's all right. It's just the quietness this weekend, knowing nothing is going to explode between them. I'm looking forward to him being away. I think it'll be good for all of us.'

Her voice trailed off. Her eyes were still closed. I sipped my drink and thought about the previous evening. I despised myself for what I'd done. It was so juvenile, the kind of thing Kevin and myself did as children, shadowing courting couples out the roads. And now I was sitting here, having an adult conversation with the girl I'd spied on. I couldn't be her friend and be a voyeur at the same time. That was all part of what was expected of growing up, wasn't it, the ability to leave behind the things that needed leaving?

'Right,' Hannah said. 'Let's go.'

'Where to?'

'Kilkea, Levitstown, Maganey, Carlow, Knocknagee and home.'

'Jesus, that's twenty miles.'

'Are you up to it?'

And she was gone, one foot on the pedal, gliding out of the pub yard, turning left and speeding away from me. I followed at a distance, watching her. Blue jeans, blue shirt, black hair in streamers behind her.

We went back along the road we'd come, through Levitstown and down into Maganey, on into Carlow and into Castledermot. It was seven o'clock when we reached my house.

'You hungry?'

'Famished.'

'Well, cone on in.'

We left the bikes in the yard and went inside. My father was sitting at the table, reading the papers.

'And how was the cycle?'

'Don't ask,' I said. 'It was more like a forced march.'

'He's not fit,' Hannah said.

'If you shut up, I'll feed you. Otherwise nothing.'

We sat at the table, the three of us, laughing and eating.

'Kevin not about?' my father asked.

'He's in Dublin, with my aunt, he's coming down on the early bus in the morning.'

'Might as well. Break the monotony. And that's what I'm going to do myself. Do you know where I'm going?'

I shook my head.

'I'm going out to Davy Walsh for a game of meggars. I haven't played meggars in twenty years.'

'Good on you,' Hannah laughed.

I followed my father into the yard and waved him off.

'Don't strain your shoulder now.'

'Divil a chance.'

When he'd gone, I went back inside. Hannah was washing the dishes.

'I'd have done that.'

'But you're knackered,' she said, flicking me with the tea towel.

I tidied the table.

'So what are you doing for the rest of the night?'

'Nothing. Am I holding you up, is there some young one waiting for you down the Laurels?'

'Not that I know of.'

'Do you want to go for a walk or something? It's a shame to be in on a night like this.'

'Fine. But no bikes.'

'No bikes.'

We walked down the lane, past Hannah's house. Her father was in the yard.

'Everything all right?' he shouted.

'Yeah. We're just going down the low farm for a walk.'

He waved us on.

'See, sometimes things can be normal.'

We crossed two fields, coming down to a small clump of trees on a slight incline. We sat there, looking across the fields we had just walked, back along the lane to the farm buildings.

'What happened to your man, the guy from Athy?'

'He's past tense,' Hannah said. 'Since yesterday. I thought you'd know that.'

'What do you mean?'

'I saw you. On Rice's Hill.'

'Fuck. I'm sorry.'

She laughed. 'No you're not, you enjoyed being a peeping Tom.'

'Fuck, fuck,' I stuttered. 'No. I am sorry. I was thinking about it all the time, today. It was really childish. Honest to God, I'm sorry, Hannah.'

'It's okay, you didn't cramp my style or anything. I wasn't interested anyway, I was just waiting for him to go.'

'Did he know I was there?'

'He did not, are you mad? I just saw you, making your escape.'

'I feel like a complete eegit.'

'Because you got caught?'

I felt myself blush.

'You're an oddball.'

'Am I?'

'Yeah, sort of.'

'It just happened,' I said. 'I didn't set out to follow you. I just saw you in the Rocks and did it, on an impulse. But I am sorry. I hope it doesn't fuck things up. You know.'

'Would I have asked you to go out today if it did?' Hannah smiled.

'I suppose not.'

'You just couldn't resist me, I suppose. I was wondering if you'd say anything and then I wondered when I'd get my chance to say something. It was a long wait.'

'I'm sure it was.'

'I hope no one followed us here,' Hannah said and, as she spoke, she turned and kissed me. That kiss was a release, the shock and tension flowed out of me.

'You're forgiven.'

'Thanks.'

We kissed again, a deeper kiss. I put everything else out of my head and went with that moment. With the smell of her hair, the hardness of her tongue inside my mouth. I hugged her and inhaled her perfume, her taste, the softness about her. And, then, without warning, the tears came. I couldn't stop myself. My body convulsed and something from a very long time ago swept over me. I clung to Hannah. She stopped kissing, just cradled me to her, letting my body wear itself out, waiting till I had no tears left to cry, till I was exhausted.

'I'm sorry.'

'It's okay. Is it you and Kevin?'

'No,' I said. 'Something just came back to me. I haven't been hugged by a woman since I was a small kid. It was like, when you hugged me, like I remembered something from way back. My mother tucking me into bed. That feeling, the way I'd smell her hair. I don't know . . . something. Jesus, I feel really stupid.'

'It's okay.'

'It was you that reminded me one time that you're only a year older than me. I didn't mean to make you into a mother figure.'

Hannah laughed, quietly. 'I don't think we were headed in that direction, do you?'

'No.'

She put my head on her lap and stroked my hair.

'I remember when your mother died. She was the first person I knew who died. I remember your father coming into our kitchen and telling my mother and she started crying. It was February. I was just in from school, I still had my coat and scarf on. Kevin was in the sitting room, watching telly. She sent me down the field to get my father. It was fierce cold. When he got back my father shook your father's hand and then my mother got into your father's car and they drove down the lane. Jesus, I remember that as clear as anything.'

'Clearer than I do,' I said but Hannah didn't seem to be listening. She shivered, in spite of the heat.

'And I remember you in the graveyard. You were wearing a denim jacket, the one with the fur inside. You were so pale. I was standing across from you. I thought you were going to faint.' She turned to me. 'Jesus, Tim, your mother was fabulous-looking, wasn't she?'

I nodded.

'I thought she was the most beautiful woman I ever saw. I remember wondering, after she died, if I could ask your father for a blue dress she had. I thought it was the most wonderful thing I ever saw. I remember all that so clearly and I hardly remember my own mother's funeral at all. Isn't that strange?'

And then she was silent and I had nothing to say. I reached up and combed her hair with my fingers. She smiled for a second and then she was gone again, back to that bleak afternoon in Coltstown Cemetery.

I closed my eyes and, for a long time, I listened to the evening.

'We're a right pair, aren't we?'

I looked up. Hannah was smiling down at me. 'Sitting

here, being maudlin, on a fine night, with a big fat moon rising. Are you all right? I'm not helping, talking about your mother like that.'

'No, I'm glad you did. I never think about that. I put it all away. My father never talks about her either and I know it still gets to him, even now.'

'What age was your mother when she died?'

'Thirty-two. They were married when she was twenty. My father was twenty-five. She was twenty-two when I was born. She'd only be forty now.

And then we were quiet again and some of the light went from the day and the moon rose up over us and threw shadows that were as sharp as the shadows carved by the sun. We stayed there, in the half darkness of that stand of trees. A fox crossed the bottom of the field. I nudged Hannah. She nodded. We watched him, red in the white light, flowing through the grasses and away through a gap in the hedge. And still we sat in silence, the moon climbing higher, the shadows of the trees shrinking until the light was directly above us.

'I suppose we better go,' Hannah said. 'Work tomorrow, for some.'

Walking back across the field, I said: 'You like blue, don't you?'

'Yeah, I do,' Hannah said. 'It's my favourite colour. So you do notice some things.'

When we reached the gate of Bracken's yard we stopped. The light from the kitchen window made a shape on the dry stones.

'Will you leave my bike back down tomorrow?'

'Sure.'

'Thanks for coming out for the cycle.'

'It was a lovely day and, listen, thanks for not losing the head about yesterday. I'm sorry, dead sorry.'

'Can I kiss you again?'

'Course.'

Hannah took me into the shadow at the gable end of the house, her arms tight around my neck, her body close against me. There was a kind of desperation about us, not wanting to go but knowing the day was over. And then she stepped away from me and kissed my cheek once and was gone.

I heard the front door open and close. I walked a few yards and stopped and looked back. Through the kitchen window I saw Hannah at the sink, filling a kettle with water. I waved, though I knew she couldn't see me. I woke the following morning, just after five. It was broad daylight but it wasn't the brightness that had wakened me. I'd come awake suddenly and I lay in bed, aware that something was wrong, something inside me had shaken me out of my sleep. I was uneasy but I couldn't fathom why. It had nothing to do with what had happened the night before, it wasn't guilt. But something was ringing a bell in my head, something had made me anxious. And so, I lay there, trawling through everything that had happened the day before but nothing surfaced and I drifted back to sleep and then, as suddenly as the first time, I was awake again and the phrase was ringing in my head.

'Is it you and Kevin?'

That's what Hannah said. What had she meant by that? Was it just a phrase in passing or did she know something about us and, if she did, how had she found out? I looked at the clock, ten past six. I got out of bed, afraid I'd fall asleep again, and pulled on my clothes. Downstairs, I made some tea and leafed through the previous day's paper, waiting for it to be seven o'clock. I knew Hannah walked down to meet the bus at half-past. I wanted to be at her gate when she came out. I needed to know what she'd meant.

My father came down at ten to seven.

'You're up with the lark!'

'Couldn't sleep. I'm just going out for a walk.'

'Right. I'll probably be gone by the time you're back. I'll see you this evening.'

'Yeah.'

I left the house and turned on to the lane. The morning was already hot, the poppies in the ditches fresh and red after the night. I walked fast, I wanted to catch Hannah as soon as she appeared, to get enough time to talk to her before she caught the bus.

At the end of the lane, I sat on the top bar of a wooden gate, across from Bracken's yard. The house seemed asleep. The minutes dragged by. Ten past seven, a quarter past. I wondered whether she'd slept it out, whether she wasn't going to work. My stomach was churning. And then, before I knew it, the door was open and she was in the yard, a bag over her shoulder.

I jumped down and went to meet her.

'Jesus, are you here all night?' she laughed.

I fell in beside her.

'You're up early.'

'Couldn't sleep.'

'Was I that good?'

'Hannah, there's something I have to ask you about, something you said last night.'

'Yeah, what?'

'You asked me, when I started crying, if it was because of Kevin and me.'

'Ah hah.'

'What did you mean?'

'What I said. Was it because of you and Kevin, because of whatever's between you two?'

'Yes but what . . .'

'I don't know what, Tim. I just presumed there's something between you. You're always together and I've never seen either of you with a girl. That's all. I took it for granted you two were more than just good friends. I thought it might have something to do with that. Had it?'

'No.'

'But there is something?'

'Sort of. It's just messing. Just finding out, you know? Just something new.'

'You don't have to tell me about it. It has nothing to do with me.'

'Yeah but last night had something to do with you, with both of us.'

'Maybe you didn't enjoy it?'

'No, I did.'

'So did I, it's the same as you and Kevin, it's enjoyable and exciting for me. Isn't that okay?'

We were almost at the top of the lane. I half expected to hear the factory bus revving down the street.

'Yes, of course it is, I had a good time. Yesterday was a great crack. It was one of the best days I've had.'

'Well then we must do it again sometime.'

'Yes.'

'Look, Tim, what you and Kevin do is your business and what we do is our business. I'm not telling you what you should or shouldn't do. I enjoyed yesterday, too. We can talk about this again.'

'I just wondered why you said that, what you knew.'

'Well, I didn't follow you. Maybe I will some day.'

'Don't be like that,' I said.

'It's a joke, Tim, just a joke. Lighten up.'

We sat on the wall at the side of the road.

'I just don't want to turn around to Kevin and tell him I don't care about how he feels. It took a lot for him to tell me and then it just, kind of, happened between us.'

'And is that how you feel?'

'Like I told you, it's just a chance for excitement. I didn't see anything wrong in it.'

'It's just sex.'

'Yeah.'

'Well, then, that's okay as far I can see, isn't it? Just like the stuff we did when we were kids.'

'I suppose so. For me. It might mean more to Kev.'

'It might but then we could have ended up having sex last night. Would that have been okay?'

I nodded.

'And maybe we will. Don't get all worried about it.'

'Yeah but Kev . . .'

'You and Kev do what you do. You and me are something different. It's not a life sentence or anything, you know. Enjoy it, Tim, there's enough misery around us.'

'Is it as simple as that?'

'The way I see it, it is. Now, here's my bus.'

She jumped down from the wall and swung her bag over her shoulder.

'We'll talk, all right. As much as you like. Mind yourself.'

The bus creaked to a halt. A few women banged on the windows and waved to me.

'Had you that poor young fellow up riding all night, Hannah?' one of them shouted.

'Jealousy, Nan, jealousy.'

And then the bus was gone.

I went back in home and made some breakfast. I wasn't all that much clearer in my head. All I knew was that the weekend had been a good one, that Hannah and myself had got on better than I'd ever imagined, that she wasn't shocked or outraged by anything – neither my watching her on Rice's Hill nor what she knew of Kevin and me. I could talk to her and there was an air about her, a devil-may-care attitude that was less threatening than Kevin's. Little by little this had been building, from our talk in the lane a week before, from what I'd seen two days earlier, from what had happened the day before, it had been building to a time, this time, when I wanted to be with Hannah, to enjoy myself with her. But I suspected Kevin wouldn't take kindly to what had happened. I doubted if he'd be as understanding of me and Hannah as she was of him and me. And I knew I'd never dare tell him.

Why did I feel I was on the verge of betraying something between us? There was no betrayal. It was like Hannah said, just a time to enjoy ourselves. It was all okay. And then there was a voice from the lane.

'How's it going?' Kevin, rucksack on his back, grinning in at me. 'Have you got the rashers on?'

I leaned out through the window.

'Come on in. How was Dublin?'

'Brill. We're going to love it.'

*

We talked about the future so much, in the weeks after you finished school, and I think a lot of the time we talked to give ourselves a chance to find a way to deal with the present.

You came up and worked with me, finishing off the wall, getting the garden into order. It was a poor excuse for summer last year. Only last year. It seems so long ago now. And while we worked we talked.

I wanted to sit down with your parents, tell them we'd been waiting for this chance to be together.

'You don't have to tell them,' you said. 'They know I come up here, they know you collect me, they know we knock around together. You don't need to give them every detail.'

'Maybe I should explain, you know.'

'Explain what? What is there to explain? They're not complaining. What are you going to tell them, that we've been sneaking around avoiding each other and everybody else for the last two years, that we managed to keep away from each other most of the time? Big deal!'

I saw the sense in what you said. I didn't know what I wanted to tell them or why I felt I needed to say anything, it just seemed the right thing to do. And, while we worked, you planned what you'd do with the ground around the house, the half-acre at the back and the half-acre to the side.

'We'll definitely keep the orchard. Definitely. Put in some new trees, pears, damsons, cherries in the side garden. We'll have the vegetables and stuff near the house and I'll use what's left for work. We could put in a separate gate, on to the lane. I'll have a couple of greenhouses out there.'

I'd watch you stepping out the measurements in the paddock, drawing up plans at the kitchen table, going back out when the rain cleared and checking again. We went to garages and looked at vans, got brochures, discussed the pros and cons of different models. It was part of the game, neither of us mentioned that this was all three years away.

And it went on for weeks. Working, talking, passing each other in the kitchen and stopping to kiss but, mostly, living in the future. And we both knew why. We'd spent so long doing just that, avoiding the present because there was none, that now we found it too awkward to face. It might have gone on that way, I had no means of dealing with it. You were the one who faced it down.

We'd just come back from a walk across the fields, one of the few warm evenings in that July. I filled the kettle and put it on the cooker and then went to see what you were doing. I found you in the hall, watching two butter-flies flapping against the glass and then you reached up and opened the top of the window and ushered them out into the evening. The light caught the side of your face and I saw the tracemark of a tear. You must have known I saw it because you spoke without turning.

'It's no good, is it?' you said.

'What isn't?'

'For fuck's sake, Tim, you know what. We're locked into this iceberg. The summer is shit and we spend our time talking about what we're going to do and going to do but what are we doing?'

'We're working,' I said.

'You stupid bollocks,' you said and, for the first time, I heard the real bitterness and doubt in your voice. 'Are you totally blind, deaf and dumb? Are you never going to shake yourself out of this?'

'This what?'

'This what, this what? Is that all you can say? This coldness. I've come up here every day since the exams finished, I've been here night, noon and morning and you hardly even touch me. If anyone makes a move, it's me. How often have you touched me without me making the first move?'

'I don't know,' I said. 'I haven't been keeping count.'

'Well, I have.'

'I didn't know we were into the mathematics of the relationship.'

'What relationship?'

You opened the front door and went outside and around by the gable. I waited in the hall, for you to come back. And then I saw you cycling out on to the road and I knew I had to go after you. By the time I'd got the car, and caught up with you, you were halfway home. I stopped a hundred yards ahead of you and got out.

'I'm sorry,' I said.

You got off the bike, your eyes were red.

'Just say it, will you, just say it, just let it go. I said it before, just let it go if that's what you want.'

'It's not what I want.'

'We can't stay stuck for ever, you're freezing me out.'

'I don't mean to.'

'How do I know that?' you asked.

'You know.'

'But I don't. You think I do but I don't. How could I?

All I know is what I feel. I know nothing about you at all. So how could I know how you feel?'

And you were right. I needed to break down the icicle bars around me.

'Come back home with me.'

'I don't think so,' you said and I knew you meant it.

'Please.'

'You go. I'll come and see you tomorrow.'

There was no point in arguing, you'd come if and when you were ready.

I got into the car, turned and drove back towards Castledermot. In my mirror I saw you, still standing at the roadside. You grew more and more distant but you never once turned to look after me.

I thought that was the longest night of my life. I wanted to go out, get away from the house, but I was afraid you'd ring and I'd miss you.

The next day was even longer and the rain came again. I wanted to ring you but I was afraid of what I'd hear. I imagined I might never see you again. When I think of that now I get angry with myself for ever imagining something so trite could be an adequate rehearsal for your absence from the rest of my life.

That night passed, of course it did, and so did the following day and you came back that evening and everything we had planned to say, every accusation and apology, was drowned by the passion of the silence between us.

I was upstairs, sorting through some books, and you came up without a sound, stood at the head of the stairs watching me. I don't know how long you were there before I sensed it but, as I stood up and turned, you crossed the landing. The rain was still streaming down your face, your hair ragtailed behind your ears. I lifted you on to the bed we'd lain on, talking, so many times but now the only sound was the rain battering against the window.

We undressed each other. Your skin was wet and cold, your nipples hard as frozen snow. I wanted to warm you, inside and out, to melt away the unkindnesses. That's all I had on my mind, to love you in silence. Fucking didn't come into it.

Later in the evening, when our bodies were softer, warmer, more at ease, when the urgency had gone out of us, we fucked for the first time and then we fell asleep and, when I woke, it was dark outside and the clouds were low across the fields and the rain had settled in for the night. I saw your eyes in the dimness, watching me, and, still, neither of us spoke. Instead, you slid on top of me and put me deep inside you and fucked me again, your body silhouetted against the night sky outside.

I woke sometime after two and you were gone.

Downstairs, on the kitchen table, you'd left a dark green ribbon from your hair.

*

I didn't see Hannah at all that week and I saw Kevin only once. It was partly by choice and partly by accident. Kevin was busy with his father and I was working from the Tuesday. There was nothing unusual in my not seeing Hannah, I knew that. There were times when I wouldn't see her from one end of the month to the other.

On the Thursday of that week Kevin called and we went for a ramble down the lane but we did nothing beyond talking.

'It's good to talk,' Kevin said. 'I've been thinking about this a lot, about us. I don't want you to think it's just about screwing one another. It's not. I thought about it a lot over the weekend, about knowing one another so long. It's not like just shagging someone you'll never see again. It's more important than that. It could be more of a problem.'

'How do you mean?' I asked, though I knew quite well what he meant. I wanted to hear it from his lips, to confirm my fears about what he expected of the relationship.

We were at the end of the lane, outside Kevin's yard. We turned, automatically, and walked back the way we'd come. I glanced into the yard in passing but there was no sign of Hannah.

'Well there's so much between us, going back the years, and this is something so new, completely different from anything else. I know it doesn't make us any closer but it's a more intimate thing. Loving someone like that is a new thing, a deeper thing, and it puts a strain on everything that was there before. It's the "first league out from land", isn't it? A whole new experience. I just want to be sure all the other stuff doesn't get lost. That's all.'

'Why should it?' I said.

'It just might. If sex became everything for a while then the rest of it might get left behind and we might not be able to find it when things settle down. I mean, all I thought of, the whole weekend, was us down in Mullarney and us being there again and what you said about coming to your house when you were in the bath. I saw how easy it would be for it all to drift away from the ordinary things.'

'Well that's up to us then, isn't it, not to get tied up in that, to keep things normal.'

'Yeah,' Kevin laughed, 'but weren't you thinking about it, too? Admit it, you were.'

There was such a brightness in his voice, such an enthusiasm, that I didn't dare contradict him and, anyway, in a way he was right. There had hardly been a time in my life when I'd thought more about sex than the previous weekend. What else had been on my mind? Little or nothing, between thinking of what Kevin and I had done and spying on Hannah and then spending the day with her, I'd been in a constant state of anticipation.

We reached the head of the lane and turned again.

'Yeah, you're right,' I said. 'And you're right about the rest of it, about not getting everything tied up in sex.'

'I'm not suggesting we live celibate lives!'

'I know that.'

'Fact is, I have something in mind for the weekend. You're not working Saturday, are you?'

'No.'

'Good, there's somewhere I want to bring you.'

'Sounds intriguing.'

'It will be. Somewhere I went with the old bollocks yesterday but I won't let that spoil it for me. Are you on?'

'Sure.'

On the Friday, Hannah rang me at lunchtime, at work. 'I didn't want you to think I was avoiding you,' she said. 'I've been busy, getting stuff ready for the holidays and with work and all.'

'When are you off?'

'Monday week.'

'Right.'

'What are you doing the weekend?'

'Well, ah, Kevin wants me to go somewhere with him on Saturday. I don't even know where.'

'That's okay. And Sunday?'

'Nothing, as far as I know.'

'Do you want to go for a cycle or something?'

'Yeah, sure, it's just . . .'

'I won't say anything to him, if you think that's the best thing.'

'I do. Just at the minute.'

'Talk to you on Saturday night. Aren't you the lucky sod, screwing the whole family!'

And then she hung up. I was half-excited, half-annoyed by her remark but mostly it made me feel uneasy.

'Are they queueing for you?' the headwaiter asked, when I got back to the restaurant.

'Yeah,' I snorted, dismissively.

'Go for it, says bollocky Bill. Life's erection does not last.'

I spent a long time that day thinking about the situation. And about Hannah. I couldn't figure her out. On the one hand, she was warm, listening and helping out when she could. But there was a hardness about her, too, a cynicism that didn't sit with the softness. But the longer I thought about it the more I realized my unease stemmed from what Hannah had said on the phone, about screwing the family. Was it a joke or a barb for my benefit? If it was, I deserved it. She was right, I was playing both sides. The choice was mine. I could tell Kevin or, at least, put an end to his expectations of me. Or I could tell Hannah that I didn't see any point in what we were doing.

But what were we doing? Very little, I told myself. Just knocking around, putting in some time. In ten days she'd be in Spain and I'd be the last thing on her mind.

And, anyway, Sunday was just a day out.

And then I thought of us lying in the trees, so easy together, as if we'd been that easy all our lives and I knew I wanted that again. I wanted the softness of her body. I wanted her to hold me, to tell me what she wanted to do.

How could I explain all that to Kevin? What was it he'd said? 'The first league out'. That's how he saw it. How was I going to tell him I wanted it all to stop? I had no idea and I didn't want to think about it.

The best thing, I told myself, was to let things go and see what came of it all. I didn't like what I was doing but I didn't feel I could do anything else. I wrapped my doubts in clichés, let sleeping dogs lie, better the devil you know, and put them to bed.

> 'And the phone it never rang,
> and the old man never sang,
> and the phone it never rang the whole day long.'

We were freewheeling down Mullaghcreelan Hill, Kevin and me. He was ringing his bicycle bell and bellowing his song.

> 'And the letter never came,
> the world forgot his name,
> and the letter never came the whole day long.'

Kevin swooped ahead of me, his arms thrown wide to the sunlight and the road ahead.

'You miserable bastard,' he shouted. 'You can't touch me now. I'm free. So good luck and fuck you.'

Cycling behind him, I was frightened by the intensity Kevin was injecting into this day. That's all it was, a day out, a couple of hours away from the farm. At least that's all it was for me.

I caught up with him at Kilkea church. 'Take it easy,' I said.

'Why should I?'

'It's just a day out. The higher we fly the harder we fall.'

'Crap. The Shoebox Shitters don't recognize that kind of philosophy. I'm free of the old bastard. I didn't even ask him if I could head off today. I told him. I fucking made a point of telling him and that was it. I'm gone and the great thing is that he knows it. He knows I'm gone and he's trapped.'

'But what if something goes wrong, Kev? What then?'

'Things don't go wrong, compadre. We make them go wrong or we don't. And I don't. I got a good horse under me and the western sky stretched out before me and I'm riding. Are you coming with me?'

There was laughter in his eyes but there was a black seriousness, too.

'Sure thing, pardner. Move them out. Take them to Missouri.'

I whistled and Kevin whistled and we picked up speed and went on.

Enjoy yourself, I told myself. Things are coming out all right. And they were. The day before, my father had asked me if I wanted to borrow the car on the Sunday, he was going to a football match. I'd rung Hannah at work and told her. Arranged to meet her at the other end of the village after lunch on Sunday. And I'd told Kevin I'd be away, visiting my aunt in Tullamore. Everything had fallen into place.

That's what happens when you let things run their course, I told myself, when you don't go out halfway to meet your problems.

We stopped in Athy and had some tea.

'We better not stay too long here,' Kevin laughed. 'Someone might recognize me from my disco days.'

'So, where are we headed?' I asked.

'You'll like it. Trust me.'

'Give me a clue?'

'We're halfway there.'

'That tells me a lot. Nine miles gone, nine miles to go. Let me guess, we're going to turn around and go home again?'

'Nice one. Come on. Wagons ho!'

We took the Monasterevin road out of the town, following the river for a mile or so, until it twined away to our left. On through Kilberry and then we picked up the canal, for another half-mile before cutting across country and through a belt of evergreens and out into the rusty flatness of the bog.

'Down here.'

Kevin wheeled off the narrow road and on to a dry track that ran along the edge of another belt of firs. We cycled to the end of the track and came face-to-face with a mountain of peat moss.

'This is where we leave the horses and take to the desert on foot,' Kevin said, swinging off his bicycle and pushing it into the shelter of some bushes. I left mine beside it and turned to look across the miles and miles of, apparently, uniform turf.

'I was out here last week, with the old bastard, getting turf. Isn't it brilliant?'

'It is,' I said. 'Brilliant.'

Away to our left, figures moved slowly, cutting and stacking turf from the banks that were lost in the opaqueness of the landscape.

Kevin went back to the bikes and took the plastic lunch bags from the carriers.

'We might as well eat now, save us dragging the bags across the bog.'

'Where are we headed?'

'Over there,' he said, pointing vaguely to the right.

We sat in the shelter of the trees and ate our sandwiches.

'I was never out on the bog before,' I said.

'You'll love it.'

We finished our food and set off.

The apparent uniformity turned out to be stretches of peat broken, at regular intervals, by drains. The sun was directly above us and the water and peat splashed the heat back in our faces. We walked for several miles across this spongy landscape and then, in the distance, a lake appeared. I pointed it out to Kevin.

'Plastic sheeting,' he said. 'I should have let you run across and jump into it. The ultimate mirage!'

'Thanks.'

We moved on to the rails of a disused narrow-gauge line, the sleepers rotting into the turf around them, the iron rails pulped by the heat and rain of decades, melting back into the earth. I was reminded of the bikes at the gable end of Kevin's house but I said nothing.

'See, that's where we're headed.' Kevin stopped and pointed to a building on the horizon.

'Rivetting.'

'Just wait and see. And it's isolated. And you can see for miles in every direction. No chance of being surprised.'

'There'd be no chance of being surprised in my house, either.'

'Ah, yeah, but this will be an experience you'll remember all your life.'

We went on, the heat shimmering off the bog, white cotton stalked across our path, the distant building seeming never to come nearer.

'You sure that place isn't moving with us?'

Kevin didn't answer.

We crossed two more drains and, suddenly, the shed was in front of us. To its left was the outline of a wall with a window still set in it and behind this three balls of gleaming silver.

'What the hell's that?'

'Surprise number one. Wait and see.'

I hurried to get to the buildings and, as I did, I saw the source of the fire. Behind the window, still suspended in the skeleton of a small shed, were three gleaming steel basins, hanging from the slenderest of bars, the sun reflecting off them, creating hanging balls of silver fire in the afternoon light.

I followed Kevin around the outline of the structure.

'Now, look from here.'

And the sight was stunning. Three metal basins hung in mid-air and behind them a window, without glass, like a frame around the landscape, a wash of halftones and the brushwork of generations of turfcutters, the surreal and the impressionist melded together.

'We should have brought a camera.'

Kevin shook his head. 'Hah. If we did, what would this be? A photograph. It'd be like admiring a tiger and then stuffing him on your wall. It'd be ruined. Anyway, that's not all. Come here.'

We skirted the large shed that backed on to the ruined wash-house.

'We'll come back to that. But look over here.'

Crossing a rug of heather, stitched with white bog-cotton, we came on to a small patch of turf. At the end of this, two feet below us, was a pool, eight or ten feet long and six feet wide.

'It's deep,' Kevin said. 'But it's clear and it's safe, if you don't drown!'

He looked around him. 'And the desert is empty,' he said, beginning to undress, scattering his clothes before jumping into the bog pool. He sank through the water, turned and arrowed back to the surface, shaking the water from his hair, laughing. 'Are you just a spectator?'

I started to undress, Kevin lay back, watching me, and then I jumped in beside him.

The water was warm. We swam from end to end of the pool, corkscrewing down through the brown water, coming back into the light and diving again. I was exhilarated. Kevin swam up and back, in great, strong strokes before pulling himself onto the bank.

'I want to show you something else.'

I climbed out after him. He crossed the heather and went into the wooden shed. I followed, glancing uneasily across the miles of bog but they were empty. Inside, the shed was hot. A drizzle of light came through the holes in the sheet-metal roof. A few home-made wooden benches stretched the length of the walls. At the far end, three steps led to a wooden platform. I followed Kevin on to it. It was covered with jute sacks. Kevin lay down and I lay beside him. The shed smelled of heat and turf mould and sacking.

'I've waited for this,' Kevin said. 'Since I was out here. I wanted to bring you here. It's not as special as Mullarney but it's beautiful.' He kissed me. 'I want you.'

He slid along my body, still wet from the swim, kissing me as he went, until his lips closed around my prick. I froze but he didn't seem to notice, his tongue licking me, his lips sucking. I rolled on to my side, watching him, my finger tight in his wet hair, trying not to come but I couldn't stop myself.

'I'm coming,' I whispered.

But he didn't stop.

'I'm coming, Kev, I'm coming,' I said again.

He reached up and took my hand, pressing it tightly. I lay back and came, his tongue gliding along my prick. Came and came until I was drained. And then I eased Kevin onto his back and knelt above him, kissing his mouth, tasting myself from his tongue, before I took him in my mouth, until he came, until I tasted him in my throat, until I was horny again, coming again, my eyes closed, sweating, till I collapsed beside him, our skins flooding together in the heat of the dead afternoon, the motes from the sacks settling slowly about us while our breathing eased and the sweat dried on our backs and something that passed for sleep came over us.

Lying there, half-aware of the heat warping the tin roof, I wondered what would happen if someone discovered us there. I imagined a group of turfcutters walking into the shed, their heavy boots muffled in the brown snow of the bog, throwing their lunch bags into a corner, looking around for a place to light a fire, to make tea, seeing us sprawled on the sacks on this small platform. What would they make of us?

'Penny for them?' Kevin said.

I told him what I'd been thinking.

'They'd beat us to pulp,' he said, quickly.

'Why?'

'Because there'd be nothing else for them to do. They could hardly sit there and wait for us to walk out past them, could they?'

'Why not?'

'Because that's the way it is. It'd be the natural thing for them to do, to beat the fuck out of us. They'd feel they'd done their duty, taught us a lesson. And they'd be satisfied, so the next time they went swimming together and saw one another's arses or pricks they could remember us and dismiss any feelings they might have in that direction. It'd be a kind of lesson to us and a reminder to themselves.'

'You've thought about all this, haven't you?'

He nodded. 'Have you?'

I shook my head.

'I really don't think you're a real queer, at all,' Kevin laughed.

'Maybe I'm not,' I said, hoping he heard the doubt in my voice.

'But you're okay, you're doing well.' He laughed again and took my hand and kissed it. 'What if we were always together? What if we grew up together, loved one another, stayed together all our lives, lived together as old men? Imagine that. Lovers all our lives, for all our lives. Wouldn't that be something?'

He turned on his side and looked at me, his eyes dark sparks among the shadows in the shed. 'Wouldn't it?'

'Yeah.'

'I'm frightening you. It's just imagination. Like you and the men coming in here and what they might do. Just imagination, that's all.'

'But you've thought about it,' I said.

'About what?'

'About everything. About what they might do, about why they'd do it, about the future, about us. You've thought about all these things.'

'That doesn't mean they'll happen. Don't let it frighten you. It's just a daydream.'

He jumped up.

'Come on, last one in is a turfcutter.'

And then he was gone, springing down from the platform, racing through the shed, his skin lightening and shining as he ran from the shadow into the sunlight, not bothering to look as he galloped across the bog and disappeared into the water.

I followed, slowly, checking the countryside around us before venturing out. Only then did I run, letting sun and wind dry me thoroughly before diving, again, into the water.

We stayed on the bog late into the evening, swimming, talking, lying in the sun, enjoying the freedom and our own daring, walking around the place naked. I reminded Kevin of our games on Rice's Hill, as kids.

'It was all there in the stars,' he said.

We watched the sun easing itself, gingerly, over the end of the Laois hills.

'Don't be put off by things I say, I just say what I'm thinking. But don't stop me saying them. I don't want to feel I have to have secrets with you. I never had about anything else, I don't want to have now. When I have these dreams I want to tell you about them. That's all they are, for now, I know that. Maybe that's all they'll ever be. But I want to tell you about them. Okay?'

'Sure,' I said.

The sun was gone, the sky a greeny blue.

'You hungry?'

'Ravenous.'

'Let's wait till the moon comes up, then we'll go.'

'Fine.' I wanted to make something up to Kevin, for putting a damper on his enthusiasm and because I felt guilty. Already, I was thinking ahead to the following day, to Hannah.

'Why don't we have another swim?' I said. 'Moonlight madness.' I took Kevin's hand and we ran across the turf, jumping together into the pool, still holding hands, only letting go as we hit the water. I let myself sink, it was darker now, no light to break the brownness. I sank, tumbled, turned and came up, catching Kevin as I did, holding onto him, our wet mouths kissing, our bodies hardening together, scrambling out of the water, falling on the bank, coming again and then rolling together off the bank, bodies flat against the water, splashes echoing across the night.

'Look,' I said. The half-moon had come up. We lay on our backs in the water, watching it climb, and then we got out, collected our clothes and began walking back across the bog, letting the night air dry us, stopping occasionally to glance back at the shed and the outline of the sinks, kissing, laughing, finally falling silent, walking naked over the flat earth, only dressing when we reached the bicycles and then cycling slowly to the main road. We were almost in Athy before either of us spoke.

I cycled methodically, tired and hungry. It was Kevin who broke the silence. 'Chips, fish, tea.'

'Sounds good.'

'One mile away. Stay in the saddle.'

'I will.'

And then he began singing, again. Quietly.

> 'And the phone it never rang,
> and the old man never sang,
> and the phone it never rang the whole day long.'

I laughed to myself. 'Another number one for the Shoebox Shitters.'

*

I remember two afternoons, you and me at the head of the lane, one in the spring, one in early summer, the weekend before your exams began.

On the afternoon in February we took my father's old binoculars and walked to the first gateway and leaned on the gate and focussed the glasses on the Wicklow Mountains. The snow was doubled and folded in the creases of the foothills. Higher up, the rocks and crevices were painted a flat white. The wind coming across the fields chilled us. You tightened my scarf and pulled my wool hat down over my ears.

'Got to keep my baby warm.' You went back to scanning the mountains.

'Feels like I could reach out and take a fistful of snow,' you said. 'And stuff it down someone's back.' You put the binoculars in their case.

'Who owns this land?'

'Brackens. It belonged to Eddie Bracken, he died in nineteen-ninety.'

'So, who has it now?'

'It's let. Des Robinson took it. The house is locked up. It was left to Hannah Bracken but she's living in England.'

'Wouldn't it be good if we could get this field, sometime? What's in it?'

'About two acres.'

'We could put the glasshouses in here, leave the half-
acre at the side for ourselves. Have my stuff here, across
the lane, near enough but separate from the house.
Wouldn't that be good?'

'Yes, it would.'

'Could you get in touch with this woman?'

'I'm sure I could. Can we hold fire on it, till the summer?'

'Course. But the sooner we enquire the sooner we'll
know and the longer we'll have to beat the price down!'

I remember the way you grinned at me.

Always planning ahead, always leapfrogging to the
time when all the fences were cleared and we were
together.

The other afternoon, early this summer, the weekend
before your exams, we stood at the same gate, watching
three planes from the air-corps, doing their loops and
turns in the high blue sky. You followed them with the
binoculars, lost in their aerobatics. I was lost, too, watching you.

And then you took the glasses down and turned to me
and the planes were forgotten. 'This time two years I'll be
getting ready for my finals.'

'I know.'

'You should enquire about this place.'

'I will,' I said. 'I promise, I'll write to Hannah.'

'Do you know her well?'

'I used to. We grew up together.'

'Oh, I thought she was middle-aged,' you said.

'She is, she's thirty, a year older than me.'

'Sorry.'

Maybe she is middle-aged, I thought. I hadn't seen her since her father's funeral. In four years she might have become middle-aged. So might I.

'Were you close?'

I shrugged. 'Her brother and myself were closer, we were in the same class in school.'

'And where's he?'

'He died.'

'Oh.'

'It's a story,' I said, 'I'll tell you sometime. It's a long story, messy.'

'Tell me now.'

'Not now,' I said. 'But I will tell you. It's just not a very nice story.'

'Did she have your baby?' you asked, your eyes twinkling.

'No, nothing as simple as that. It had more to do with Kevin, really, her brother. I will tell you. I want to. It's part of the past you're always trying to get out of me.'

'Did he have your baby?'

'That's a bit nearer the mark,' I laughed.

'Ooooow, if only we'd known that in school, think of all the homework we could have blackmailed you out of giving.'

You put your arm through mine, rubbing your face against my shirt.

'Like I said, it got kind of messy. I will tell you. But not now.'

*I looked at my watch and turned back the way we'd
come. 'Now it's the end of playtime, back to your books.'*
'Yes, teacher,' you said, pouting and kissing me.

*

I made sure not to think at all about the previous day. I
didn't look back, I put everything that had happened on
the bog, the sex and the conversation and the beauty of
the place, out of my head and made myself busy that
Sunday morning.

We cooked, my father and I, with the kitchen doors and
windows open. We brought the table out to the yard and
ate in the shade of the wall. We were finished by twelve
and I drove him to the Square, to meet the football bus.

'I'll probably take a spin to Tullamore,' I told him.

'You'll call to Ellen?'

'Sure.'

'She'll be delighted. Her favourite nephew. Tell her I
might get down next week. Damn it, tell her there's a bed
here for her. Remind her. It'd be great to see her.'

'I will.'

'Are you going on your own?'

'Hannah might come.'

'You like her.'

'I do.'

'She's sound. I always thought.'

'Yeah, she is, yeah.'

'Right. Sure I'll see you when I see you so. I'll be back
around seven. But I'll see you whenever.'

'We won't be too late.'

I dropped him on the Square. The bus was already there, white flags drooping limply from the windows, crowds of people standing, shirt-sleeved, on the path, waiting till the last minute to get on to the stuffy bus.

'I hope we win.'

'I hope we play well. One thing at a time.'

Driving home, I kept an eye out for Kevin but there was no sign of him. I sat in the orchard, reading the papers, not thinking back and not thinking ahead. That was the way I wanted it. Compartmentalized. Safer that way, much safer.

I saw Hannah as she passed the house at twenty to two. I called to her, from the yard.

'You going somewhere?'

'Yes, I'm going up the town to meet you.'

'It was kind of stupid of me, wasn't it?'

'I thought so but . . .' she shrugged and followed me into the house. 'Where are we going?'

'How do you fancy a run to Tullamore? I thought I might give my aunt a shout. After that we can go wherever you like. I told my father we'd drop in on her.'

'Did you tell him I was going?'

'Yeah, course.'

'Very daring of you.'

I took my jumper from a chair. 'Let's go.'

We drove with the car windows open, with the radio on, drove fast. I was uneasy. I wanted to get the business of the journey over, call to my aunt, have a cup of tea and get away again.

The towns and villages passed in a glaze of children with ice-creams and open car doors and old men sitting in their gardens with radios playing.

'Did you have a good day yesterday?'

I nodded.

'Where'd you go?'

'Why?'

'Just wondering. No harm in that.'

'We cycled out to Kilberry, walked across the bog. It was nice.'

'I'm sure it was.'

'Meaning?'

'Meaning nothing. You're losing your sense of humour, Tim.'

'Am I? Maybe I am. It's difficult.'

'Only if you let it.' Hannah stretched back, her left arm dangling through the open window, a hint of perfume on the air.

'It is, though,'

'I know. Take it easy.' She put her hand on my shoulder, massaging the side of my neck, tucking her leg under her and turning to face me.

'Can I turn the radio off?'

'Course.'

'Are you happy?'

'Yes, I am.'

'Good. That's it then. Enjoy yourself. Enjoy ourselves. One more week and I'll be on holidays. Wooooooooow.' She leaned through the open window, her hair pulled back off her face, the breeze taking her voice across the fields.

'Yeeeeeessssss.' And then she turned and kissed the side of my neck, 'Find somewhere to pull in, I want you to kiss me. Properly.'

I slowed the car, pulled into a gateway, turned off the engine and put the seats back. We lay there in the heat, kissing. Nothing more, just kissing, while the traffic passed.

'I like being kissed,' Hannah said. 'It's not the only thing I like but I like it. Do you?'

'I don't have a lot of experience.'

'Well I do and I like it. A lot.'

We drove on, through Portarlington, Geashill and into Tullamore.

'This time last week you were wrecked, cycling,' Hannah said. 'I think the car suits your lifestyle better.'

'Bullshit. I'm fit.'

'We'll see,' she giggled. 'We'll see how well you pace yourself.'

Ellen's house was deserted. No car. The windows closed. I went next door.

'Oh she's gone off to Galway,' the woman said. 'Went off yesterday. Back late tonight. Who will I tell her called?'

'Tim,' I said.

'Ah yes, yes, of course. From Kildare.'

'Yeah.'

'I should have known you. I'll tell her. Would you like a cup of tea?'

'No, thanks,' I said. 'We'll go on. Thanks.'

I went back to the car and told Hannah the story.

'Well then, the day's ours.'

'Yeah. Where would you like to go?'

'How about a drive in the Slieve Bloom's?'

We drove out of Tullamore and up into the mountains.

'Did you tell Kev where you were going?' I asked.

'He didn't ask. If he does I'll say I was with the girls some-where. But he won't, the only one in his world is himself.'

We parked the car and walked up through some wood-land. I asked Hannah the names of plants and trees and butterflies. There were very few she didn't know.

'You really should do something about getting out of the factory, Hannah. Go and do something you really like.'

'I'll tell you what,' she said. 'If I'm still there when you qualify, if I haven't hooked my millionaire, you can pay for me.'

'You're on,' I said. 'But you shouldn't have to wait that long. Why don't you go back and do the exams again, get the points, go to college. You could.'

She shook her head, screwing up her face in the sunlight that came, suddenly, through a gap in the branches.

'I don't think so. I'd never buckle down to it. I'll just up and go some day.'

'Well, what about the farm? Why don't you talk to your father about that? Kev has no interest.'

She shook her head, again.

'It's there. You could do it and do something else as well.'

'Anyway,' she said, skipping ahead of me. 'Let's not talk about it. No future, no past. Just us, just now. Right?'

'Right.'

'Let's go home then.'

'Why?'

'Because I don't like it here, it's the kind of place you'd find a body in the trees.'

I laughed and we turned and walked back to the car.

It was almost six when we got to Castledermot.

'Is this the end of the day?'

'No,' Hannah said.

'Have you something in mind?'

'What time's your father back?'

'About seven.'

'Well we can't really stay in your house then, can we?'

'We can if you want,' I said. 'He won't mind.'

'He might,' she giggled, raising her eyebrows. 'Why don't we leave the car, get something to eat and then go up Rice's Hill? Would you like that?'

'Bringing me back to the scene of my crime.'

'Yeah.'

My father arrived as we were finishing our meal.

'Any luck?'

'No luck. But they didn't disgrace themselves.'

I poured some tea for him.

'How was Ellen?'

'Away in Galway,' I said. 'I left a message.'

'Grand. Are you using the car?'

'No,' I said. 'We're going walking.'

'Right. I might hop over to Davy Walsh's.'

'More meggars?' Hannah asked.

'The very thing. It's all coming back to me. The simple pleasures of youth.'

'Barefoot and ragged trousered.'

'You've heard,' my father laughed.

He dropped us on his way to Foxhill. We walked down the river bank and up to Rice's Hill.

'Were you serious, what you said about the forest today?' I asked.

'Very,' Hannah said. 'Sometimes I get bad feelings about places. Do you?'

'Once,' I said. 'I was out picking mushrooms one morning. Broad daylight. I got a weird feeling, just something I didn't like. I got out of the field as fast as I could.'

'Which field was it?'

'This one,' I said, racing ahead of her, scrambling over the ditch and out of sight. She ran after me, pausing on the broken branch of a bush and jumping down into my arms.

We walked up the hill and stopped to look back, across Abbeylands and the Cavalry Field, and then turned and went into the cover of the furze bushes. Hannah led the way. 'D'you remember the crack we had here, when we were kids?'

'Yeah.'

'And catching pinkeens in Keatley's field. Do you remember that?'

'Course I do.' I didn't tell her that Kevin and I had gone fishing there so recently.

'I always remember the two of you in the river. You were always so serious about it, like everything depended on it. Like this.' She frowned and bit down on her bottom lip. 'Always trying to catch a Black Doctor or a Red Doctor.'

She took my hand and we slid down into the hollow where I'd watched her eight days before. 'And, no, I don't always bring guys here,' she said.

'Never crossed my mind.'

She sat on the grass. I knelt in front of her.

'Just so you know,' she said. 'And I've never screwed anyone. You know, completely.'

'Neither have I.'

'Okay then.'

I leaned forward and kissed her, the pair of us swaying for a moment, before she fell backwards, laughing, and I fell beside her.

'How romantic can you get.'

I didn't answer, just pulled her on top of me, kissing her until neither of us could breathe, until we had to draw apart and I was looking into her eyes.

'Go on,' she whispered.

I kissed her again and opened her shirt. Her breast touched my hand, cool and firm. She rolled off me and undid my jeans. I thought of the afternoon before, of Kevin and me and what we'd done. I knew I wanted her more than I wanted him. I thought of what I'd done for him, simply out of excitement and guilt, and now I wanted to do all that for Hannah, too. But out of what? Gratitude? Affection? Hunger? Infatuation? Love? It didn't matter. Easing her back on to the grass I unzipped her jeans, trailing my tongue along her belly and between her legs. She smelled of powder and denim. I kissed her and licked her and tasted her. I buried my face between her legs, my tongue flicking. She reached for me but I was beyond her reach, her fingers twined my hair and I went on, I heard her moan and I didn't stop. The taste was different now. Her legs cradled me, moving gently with the rhythm of my tongue and, then, her hands were tight in my hair, pulling my tongue into her and she was coming, her body stiffening, holding me there, holding and then easing, easing after she'd come. I laid my face against her thigh and breathed in the scent of grass and perfume and come.

And then Hannah was lifting my head, urging me up, making a place for me between her legs.

'Just don't come in me, okay? Tell me when you're coming.'

She put me inside her. It was easy to do, we were both so wet.

'I'm coming now,' I said, immediately, easing myself out of her, rolling onto the grass, away from her. But she turned me on to my back, taking my prick in her hand, holding me till the white come pooled in her palm, watching me, never taking her eyes off me. And when I'd finished she rubbed the seed on her breasts, her hands sliding under the deep curves and onto her belly. Afterwards, we lay wrapped about each other, half-dressed, and I told her I loved her.

*

I never told you this, though some time, given time, I might have. One night, last Christmas, when we were in bed, I remembered that Sunday evening with Hannah on Rice's Hill.

It may seem strange, that a summer day from ten years before should come back to me on a winter night, but I know why it happened. I should have told you, there was no reason not to, it might have been the right time, it might have been a way to open the locked box that was part of my past. But I didn't.

It was a night in Christmas week. We were in my bed, our bed, upstairs. The light from the Christmas tree in the hall downstairs was shining in the doorway of the bedroom. There was one candle lighting on the bedside table. We were making love and you were kneeling over me, I was inside you, and you were coming. I wanted to come, too, I wanted to feel my seed scattering inside you. And, for an instant, I thought of that afternoon on the hill, when I couldn't keep from coming. But then, on that Christmas night, in our bed, in this house, the house that was almost ours, the house that will always be ours, I waited. I held your face between the backs of my hands, the way you liked me to, stroking your cheeks. Your face was flushed, your skin hot, your breasts glistening above me. You were getting closer, riding me, riding my whole body, your eyes closed, head thrown back, biting down on your lip. Coming, coming with hardly a sound. Maybe a whimper, maybe a whisper, no more than that, squeezing me into you. Coming, coming, your body arching backwards, your breasts flattening, your hair falling down your back, your face caught in the light of the candle. Back, back, your hair catching the colours from the lights of the tree. Coming as your body twisted forward, driving deeper on to me. I held myself against you and then you came and your body released me and I came on you. Afterwards, we lay in the bath together and you asked me what I was thinking about and I said: 'How I'd like to come inside you.' And that was true. Already, I'd forgotten about the summer evening a long time ago. It was part of the past then and I never imagined, in my wildest dreams, that I'd need the past or that it would become the only place in which I could love you, again.

*

I didn't know what to do, where to turn or how to get through the days of that week. I was full of regret, confusion, want and fear. I dreaded meeting Kevin, because I imagined myself telling him about Hannah and me, and I dreaded not seeing Hannah, because I wanted her.

And there was something else about that Sunday that confused me. I knew how much I needed Hannah, needed

her to listen to me, to talk to me, to reassure me. And yet,
I was the one who had taken the initiative when we made
love, that dependence had disappeared then, I'd had the
confidence to make love to her, not just to wait for her to
tell me what to do. But, now, as the week wore on, that
confidence disappeared and I had no idea how to recover
it. All I knew was that I was full of confusion. But I did
nothing about it. I let the days slide by, hiding from Kevin,
waiting for Hannah to come and find me. And all week the
desperation festered. I skulked in the fields around Brack-
en's, ducking when Kevin appeared, wishing Hannah into
the yard but never seeing her. I thought of ringing her at
work or at home but I had no idea how I could explain
things in three minutes or ten minutes. And anyway, I was
afraid she'd dismiss me, grow tired of my dependence. I
needed to see her, to know there was something between
us, needed to be face to face with her. If we were face to
face everything would be all right, I told myself.

By the Thursday, I knew I had to do something. Two
days more and Hannah would be on holiday. Gone. Out
of reach. So I went down to the house that evening. The
kitchen door was open. I knocked and walked in. Kevin
was sitting at the table, reading. 'I was just going to call
up,' he said. 'I was up to my eyes the whole week. How's
things?'

'Fine.'

'Do you want to go somewhere?'

I shook my head. 'I'm knackered. Just dropped down to
say hello.'

I paused, waiting for something but I didn't know what. 'Where's everyone?'

'He's down the low farm. Hannah's upstairs, getting her stuff together.'

'Oh yeah, she's off this weekend, isn't she?' I said, as coolly as I could.

'Yep. Do you want tea?'

'Sure.'

He filled the kettle at the sink. I thought of the night I'd stood in the lane, watching Hannah at the sink.

'I was fairly knackered myself, after Saturday,' Kevin said quietly.

I smiled.

'It was really good.'

I nodded.

He put the kettle on the cooker and came and stood behind me, his hands on my shoulders, and kissed my neck.

'Be careful.'

'I want you.'

'Can we have the tea first,' I said, trying to lighten the moment.

He kissed me again and went to get the cups.

'Will I call Hannah?'

'Yeah, do.'

I walked into the hall and up the stairs, past Kevin's room. Hannah's door was open. She was laying clothes out in neat piles on her bed. I knocked and went in.

'Hiya,' she smiled.

'There's some tea ready.'

'Great. I didn't know you were here.'

'Can we talk? Before you go away. I need to talk to you.'

'Okay. When?'

'Tomorrow night.'

'Sure. Are you all right?'

'Yes and no.'

She rubbed the side of my face. 'Missing me already?'

'Yes.'

'Yeah?'

'Yes.'

'All right. Tomorrow night. If you like, I'll cycle out to the hotel. Half seven.'

'Thanks.'

I went back down to the kitchen. 'She's on her way.'

'Heavy into the packing.'

'Yeah,' I said. 'She's lucky.'

After the tea, after the banter between Kevin and Hannah, after she'd gone back upstairs, Kevin walked down the lane with me.

'The old bastard wanted me to check on Hote, he's lame. I told him to do it himself. And he did!' There was glee in his voice. 'I told him he'd have to get used to it, that I wouldn't be here to do it for him that much longer. And when he was on the way out I told him to remind me to show him where the sewerage rods were. No more fecking about with the Shoebox Shitters,' he laughed loudly. 'And what blow have you struck for freedom this week, compadre?'

What was I to say? I made love to your sister?

'Not a lot. I worked to earn the Yankee dollar, that was it.'

'Satisfactory, compadre. It's not every day it's given to a man to break the mould.'

I didn't respond. Kevin stopped walking.

'I meant what I said, about wanting you, I just want you to feel the same way about me.' His voice dropped to a whisper. 'I've been saving my come for you.'

I turned to him. 'That's heavy talk, Kev.'

'I know. But it's true. I've been waiting all week to see you. It's six days.'

'I know that.'

'I just want to touch you again, I want you to touch me. I want to taste you. I want to come with you. It's not the same on my own.' He laughed, self-consciously. 'I'd hardly be standing here, saying this, if I didn't really mean it, would I?'

'No.'

'And I know it mightn't be the same for you, I know it doesn't have to have the intensity I feel. But I can't help that. I can't make you love me and I can't make myself not love you.'

'I do love you, Kev. I've always loved you. You know that. It has nothing to do with screwing.'

'I can't stop myself wanting to screw with you, then, is that better? I'm trying not to be too pushy, that's the real reason why I didn't go looking for you this week, I waited till you wanted to see me but it doesn't make it easier or different. When I saw you in the kitchen I just wanted to kiss you, to hold you, to feel you against me. It's not easy to say all this.'

And I knew it wasn't. I admired him for it. If I'd had a quarter of his honesty, things would have been a lot less complicated. But I didn't, not even then, so I went into a field with him, lay down in the shelter of a ditch and wanked him and then let him suck me.

I think of that now and I feel such a bastard because it had nothing to do with anything, not with love or even lust. It had to do with trying to find the easy way out, with cowardice. I thought of it when I carried Kevin's coffin. And it feels every bit as bad, every bit as nasty now as it did then. There is no redemption anywhere in that scene. It was callous.

Hannah might have tried to isolate it from everything else, she might have been able to do that, but I couldn't and I still can't. I think that was the lowest point between Kevin and me. Everything that happened after that, every deception that followed was less dishonest than what happened in that field on that night. I felt nothing for him. It was a mechanical thing. I despised myself for it. We lay in a dry dyke under the ditch, I pulled his jeans down and took his prick in my hand and wanked him. It didn't take long. I watched the seed fall on to the dusty clay between us, spurting on to the dried leaves, losing its whiteness as it seeped into the earth. And then I stood there while he took me in his mouth. I didn't even want to come, I just wanted to get finished, but I didn't stop him.

There. It was as cold, callous, hard and basic as that. No romance. No magic. And no courage to say I didn't want to do it. The easy way out. But there was nothing easy about it.

*

Your first weekend home from college. I collected you from the train in Athy. We had our tea in your house.

'You should come up here more often for your meals,' your mother said. 'We'd be delighted to have you.'

'He's a good cook,' you said.

'Yes, but still.'

'Did you want to eat in my house when we were going out?' your father asked.

Your mother smiled. Your smile.

'That's not to say you're not welcome,' he laughed.

When we got home, you pulled out a sheet of paper from your bag and spread it on the kitchen table. It was a scale map of the side garden, the half-acre that was lying untilled.

'I've been thinking about this. I think we should put in a whole new orchard from here to here, right under our bedroom window. We'll put vegetables here.' You indicated an area at the other end. 'And a small glasshouse here, for our stuff.'

I glanced over it but it was your face that fascinated me. So full of enthusiasm.

'I love you,' I said.

'I hope so. This'll cost about three hundred quid for the

trees! And we'll have to clear the scrub off. Soon. We'd really need to get these in before the end of November. Sooner if we can.'

'I still love you.'

'Well that's all right then. Can we start on this tomorrow?'

'Yes.'

'And will you get a chance to work on it this week?'

'Yes.'

'And we can get it finished next weekend and put the trees in the weekend after that?'

'Yes.'

You put your arms around me.

'Okay, you can take me to bed then.'

Later on, when we'd lit a fire, we went through the list of what we needed to buy. Apples, plums, greengage, pears, cherries, nuts, damson. You knew the varieties and where they should be planted.

'We'll have two orchards. Old and new. Let the kids worry about the next one!'

'You're right.'

*

I met Hannah outside the hotel and we walked down to the graveyard at the end of the drive. We sat on the flat stones near the ruins of the medieval church. It was a beautiful evening, a light breeze had lifted the weight of the day's heat and freshened everything.

'Looks like rain,' Hannah laughed. 'Wouldn't it be great if it rained as we took off for Spain?'

'What time are you flying?'

'Half-two. Esther's brother is driving us to the airport, they're collecting me at ten. And then up and away – sun, sand, sangria and sex! Well, that's the theory anyway. No point in denying it before we go, is there?'

'No.'

'You've a face on you that'd stop a clock.'

'Thanks.'

'It's true. Talk.'

So I talked. I told her about what had happened the previous evening. And I told her I loved her. She laughed at that. 'Don't talk about love too much.'

'Why not?'

'It's dangerous territory, Tim. You like me, okay? And I like you.'

'I like lots of people, Hannah. It doesn't mean I think about them all the time.'

'And why do you think about me all the time? Because we fit together well?'

'No. It's not just that. I love being with you, I love talking to you, I love the good feeling I get when I'm with you.'

'Do you know what that is?'

'What?'

'It's companionship and conversation and emotion. And there's more than that. There's sex. I like all those things, too, but we're into dangerous territory when we talk about love. You don't love me. You fancy me and I fancy you. If we were in love we'd be going away together tomorrow. Or staying here together. It's just foolishness because it gets in the way of the things you're talking about. It gets in the way of companionship and conversation and good times. It pulls you down. And it fucks up your head.'

'Thanks,' I said. I was devastated.

Hannah put her arms around me, pulled me towards her. I didn't try to stop her.

'Listen to me, Tim. You're getting screwed up every time you turn around. You and me get on well and that confuses you. You and Kevin have a good time and that confuses you. You're guilty about last night. Why?'

'Because I'm misleading him.'

'Maybe he doesn't see it that way.'

'He told me he's in love with me.'

'I told you. Love fucks everything up. Love is for when you need an excuse to stay with someone for the rest of your life and if Kevin doesn't see that, that's his problem, not yours or mine. He's spent his whole life carrying flags for everything and anything and once he thought they'd get on my father's nerves he flew them even higher. And love is another one. You pulled him off last night, so what? Fuck's sake, Tim, if I started worrying about love every time I pulled some guy off I'd be dead by now. Or married with six kids. Whichever is worse.'

'I don't understand you,' I said.

'Why not?'

'You talk like this and yet you can sit with me and talk about my mother and be all concerned and full of understanding.'

'So?'

'So it's a bloody contradiction.'

'Bullshit.' She stood up, her hands on her hips, her face a couple of inches from mine. 'Don't you start lecturing me, Tim. Don't fucking try it. If I was concerned it was because I was concerned. I wasn't pretending. I wasn't putting on an act for anybody. I liked your mother, I admired her, everything I said about her was true. And everything I said about everything else was true as well. I don't have to apologise to you for anything. I liked you, I flirted with you, but I never said I was going to live with you or marry you or any of that shit. If you want to be my friend, be my friend. Don't try to control me. Why do men always want to control you? If they don't want to stick their cocks down your throat, they want to drag love into it so they can keep tabs on you. And that's what you want, isn't it?'

I didn't answer her. There was nothing I could say. She was right. I did want her for myself and I wanted her to want me for herself. I needed her to provide me with the courage to tell Kevin that I wanted out. And why did I want out? Not because I had suddenly changed but simply because I wanted Hannah more than him. I preferred her company, I preferred sex with her. I was changing. I was growing out of some of the intricacies of a lifelong friendship. I was running when I wanted to walk. And I wanted

Hannah to undo all the strings for me or give me a reason to undo them.

'I'm not trying to dump you, sunshine,' Hannah said, gently. 'But I'm going away tomorrow. I'm not telling you I won't get off with fellows in Spain. I'm not telling you anything. But I won't run off with any of them. I'll be back in a fortnight. I'd like if we could keep on what we have. Your tongue is magic!'

'Okay,' I said. 'And what should I do about Kev?'

'Whatever you do, don't do it because of me. That's all I can say to you. It won't make any difference to me. Same as spending the night with some guy in Spain won't make any difference. That's the way I am, Tim. I won't push you, one way or the other. But I'm not demanding anything, either.'

I swung my legs beneath the gravestone I was sitting on. 'Famine or feast?'

'Something like that. I hope it's feast for the next two weeks.'

'Send me a card?'

'Of course I will.'

I put my hands on Hannah's waist and pulled her to me. I breathed in the cotton of her shirt and the cleanliness of the evening.

'Enjoy yourself, Tim. I keep telling you that. There's enough misery behind us and in front of us. Make an island in the Mississisery.'

We both laughed out loud.

'Keep telling you, I'm not my brother's dumber sister. Donkey Hote. Mississisery. Six of one . . .'

Hannah could do that. Leaving me laughing, put me straight, put me down, build me up, frighten me. When I talked to her, when I listened, everything she said made perfect sense. But afterwards, when I tried to put all the pieces together they never seemed to fit.

And when she was gone to Spain I didn't know what she had told me and I didn't know what I should do. Was I to use the time to tell Kevin that I didn't want to have sex with him again or was I to take whatever pleasure I could out of the weeks ahead?

I didn't want to lose Kevin, that wasn't a possibility. You don't go that far to lose somebody that close from your life. I knew that, it was written deep inside me. I gave myself a week to work things out, to deal with things inside my head and then a week to talk to Kevin. That was the plan. But that wasn't how it went. Afterwards, I told myself it wasn't my fault, but afterwards is often just an excuse.

*

I water the trees every evening now. I unroll the long hose across the yard, around by the low stone wall with the initials set at each end. I go from tree to tree, letting the water puddle around the old bark, watching the little rivers trickle down the crevices in the broken earth. And then I go back to the yard, dragging the hose behind me, and cross to the new orchard. Your orchard. And I go through the process again but more slowly. This is your garden, the seed beds near the hedge, the drills of Kerr's Pinks, the trees scattered across the half acre, the young trees from which we picked the small fruit in the early summer. I water them, I listen to the earth sucking and soughing as the night comes on.

I listen to the sound of water, I smell that particular smell of water at night. I remember us sitting in my car, listening to the water in the river. We raised so many obstacles then, when we needn't have. Now there are no obstacles at all. There is nothing between us, nothing. If you're anywhere, I tell myself, you're here, as fluid as the water round the trees, as real as the haze that comes up sometimes at dusk and stands there, inside the ditch, waiting for me to go indoors before it edges between the trees and slips up to the gate. But I wait, I stand inside the hedge and listen and I swear I hear your breathing.

*

It was Kevin who came to me. He called to the house on the Monday night. He wouldn't come in so we went walking, down the lane, past his house, across the fields. Just walking. Neither of us saying anything much. He was joking and messing, but it wasn't real, I knew that.

'I want to tell you what I think,' he said, at last.

'About?'

'Us.'

'Okay.'

'Me. I know what I am.'

'Yeah.'

'You're not so sure.'

'Maybe.'

'And I may have pushed you too fast.'

'It wasn't against my will, I didn't have to do anything.'

'But you did.'

'Yes.'

'And I don't want this friendship to go on the rocks over it.'

'Me neither,' I said, relaxing. 'I was thinking about that. Half the time, I don't know what I'm at, Kev. I just seem to stagger along, I don't know where I'm going, not the way you do. Not the way you've thought everything out.'

'That's all right but do me one favour, okay?'

'Sure.'

'If you want to screw me, if you want to do anything, just to do it, you know, no long-term stuff, tell me, do it, you start it. Don't keep it locked up, I won't think worse of you, one way or the other.'

We walked on, past the trees where Hannah and I had sat, down the field, through a gap in the ditch where we'd seen the fox.

'Some time I'd love you to make the first move,' Kevin said. His voice was low and sad.

'Maybe I will. Some time.' But that was all I said. I felt I was on more solid ground now, that something had been achieved, that Kevin recognized something, and I wasn't about to let it slip away again.

'It wasn't that I didn't care,' I said. 'Don't think that. I wanted to do it, I enjoyed it, but I don't know whether I can go on doing it, I don't have the same feelings you have.'

'I always said it, you're not a real queer.'

Kevin was laughing, I laughed too.

'Probably I'm not,'

'But it was good, it was sexy, it was exciting.'

'Yes.'

'Can I tell you something?'

'Sure.'

'First time you came in my mouth, I knew I'd never been closer to you. It was like I had your blood running in my veins. Is that weird?'

'Not weird, just very intense.'

'It was intense. It is. I can't imagine feeling that way with anyone else. Maybe I will but I can't imagine it. I'd really like that. To feel that way and know the other person felt the same. That intense.'

'There's other kinds of intensity, Kev. The last eighteen years is its own kind. It's just different. It's not any better or any worse than what you're talking about.'

'But I know the difference. I feel it. You don't.'

'That's because I'm not a real queer.'

He smiled. 'I wish you felt it.'

I do, I thought, if only I could tell you, if only I had the courage to say it straight, that I'm not gay, that I feel that way about Hannah and she's off trying to shift guys in Spain. There's the three of us on merry-go-round horses, following our dreams and unable to make any ground on them.

I was only just home that night when Kevin rang.

'We're going to be all right,' he said. 'Whatever way it goes, we're going to survive. The Shoebox Shitters will not be trifled with. The movement continues, as the bowel-doctor said to the patient.'

'Thanks, Kev.'

'It's the way it was meant to be, compadre.'

'I can't talk a lot now but I'm not saying no to everything.'

Why did I say that? Because I was horny, because I'd been thinking of Hannah as I walked down the lane and was angry that she wasn't there, because I was eighteen and I couldn't wait two weeks for something if I could have half of it tomorrow.

I went to bed feeling good, feeling I'd done something worthwhile, something that made me a different person, more grown up. I fell asleep thinking of Hannah, remembering, imagining, daring, but I dreamt of Kevin. He was happy, he was laughing. We were kids again. We were building a wall of snow against Broderick's door. It was late and dark and snowing. We rolled the snow into huge balls and piled them one on the other. When the wall was four feet high we knocked on the door and ran and hid behind the wall, lying on our bellies, peeping around the bottom of the gatepost.

Jimmy Broderick, fat and bad-tempered, opened the door and for a second we saw his face, white in the light reflected off the snow, and then the whole thing fell in across his hallway.

'Fuck, fuck, fuck, fuck.'

We listened.

'Bastards, bastards, bastards, bastards.'

We laughed.

'Fucking, fucking bastards.'

We laughed out loud and then we ran.

'He's behind us,' Kevin shouted.

I ran faster.

'He's catching us.'

Running faster.

And then Kevin stopped.

'No he's not, the fat bollocks.'

And we doubled over on the road, laughing, sweating, shaking.

'Bastards, bastards, bastards, bastards,' Kevin mimicked.

I laughed again and woke myself up, laughing out loud, tears running down my face.

I couldn't wait to see Kevin the following night, to remind him of that January when we were twelve years old.

'Bastards, bastards, bastards, bastards,' he said, like he'd stepped out of the dream.

'Do you remember his face, just before the snow fell in on him, like he was facing an avalanche in his underpants? Jesus, that was a night.'

We sat in the smoky light of the wooden loft. In the yard below, Kevin's father was changing a tyre on the car.

'Do you know what I dreamed the other night?'

'What?'

'I dreamed I was standing at the side of an open grave, that old bastard's grave,' he indicated his father. 'The whole parish was there. The coffin was in the bottom of the grave but there was no lid on it. I just stepped up to the side of the grave and pissed into it.'

'Ah, come on, tell me another.'

'I swear. It was a sweet dream.'

We lay back and listened to the sounds from the yard. Dusk was thickening. Suddenly, Kevin sat up. 'What night's this?'

'Tuesday.'

'Tomorrow's Wednesday.'

'Brilliant.'

'Bin day in Castledermot.'

'Fascinating.'

Kevin's face crumpled into a smile. 'Let's strike again, just when it's least expected. Six years later, the Shoebox Shitters return, terrorizing the Broderick ranch.'

'No snow, Kev. Third week of July.'

'Bin day, baby. Let's go.'

I scrambled down the stairs after him, out into the night, past his father and on to our bikes. I had to cycle hard to keep up with him. He turned into the village and down past Carlow Gate. Finally, I caught him as he eased up at the end of the road where Broderick lived.

'Leave your bike here.'

I did as I was told.

'Now follow me,' he said, sauntering past the line of dustbins left for the next day's collection.

We turned at the end of the road.

'Right. There's fourteen black plastic sacks. We can build a wall of plastic snow.'

It dawned on me. 'Fecks sake, Kev. If we're caught.'

'We will not be caught. We give it fifteen minutes, until it's dark, then we collect the bags, pile them high, knock the door and watch them fly, Jimmy Broderick, thigh-high in shite.'

He did a little dance.

'It's one thing when we're twelve.'

'We are always twelve, always will be. Are you in?'

'I'm in.'

We sat on the wall at Carlow Gate.

'In ten weeks we'll be in unversity,' I said. 'And here we are, piling shite outside Broderick's door.'

'But he deserves it. He's a miserable man. Mr Misery himself.'

'We laughed, sitting in the darkness, our legs dangling over the little stream beneath the wall.

'The first time I ever played football for the under-fourteens, Broderick called me a lazy fucker,' Kevin said. 'He told me I was too lazy to wipe my own arse. He shouted that from the sideline. He wasn't even involved, he just turned up to sneer. He deserved the avalanche and he deserves the wall of shite.'

'He does.'

'Time to go time.'

We walked quickly, swinging the plastic bags from the bins, hardly pausing, taking two bags in each hand, leaving them outside Broderick's gate, going back and getting another half-dozen.

'Nothing too heavy there. No danger. Just potato skins, shitty nappies, cold ashes.'

We checked the road in both directions and then moved up the garden, laying the bags sideways against the door. Five feet high, a gap for the knocker.

'Right', Kevin said, 'Light the fuse.'

He rattled the knocker, loud enough to wake the dead, and then we were running, skidding around the wall, throwing ourselves on the ground, peeping around the corner. The porch light came on. The door opened. The bags collapsed into the hall, all but two which remained against the door jamb like a drunken nun, falling around Broderick, leaving him standing in the middle. For a moment there was silence and then his high, whiny voice.

'The curse of fuck on youse.'

He tried to move forward, to get into the garden, to find the culprits. The nun collapsed, spewing tins across the porch.

'Bastards, bastards, bastards, bastards.'

We buried our faces in the clay, sputtering, edging backwards, getting past the next gate and the next before we took to our heels and ran, back to the bikes, up and away, wobbling crazily back through the village, laughing,

laughing, laughing into the night. And every now and then we'd catch our breath and one or other of us would start the cant again.

'Bastards, bastards, bastards, bastards.'

The following evening Kevin came up and hung around while my father and I finished our tea.

'Will you not eat something?' my father asked.

'No, thanks. Just had a big feed. Fish.' He giggled.

'Nice,' my father said. 'Nothing to beat fresh trout.'

'That's what we had.' He giggled again.

'You all right?' I asked.

'Grand, grand. Just a bit giddy.'

'Nothing wrong with that,' my father said.

After the meal, we went outside.

'What's up with you?'

'Brilliant idea,' Kevin said. 'Look.' He pulled a plastic bag off the carrier of his bike and opened it. Inside was a fresh trout.

'Your dinner,' I said sarcastically. 'You want me to cook it for you.'

'I had his brother for dinner. This is better. Think Jimmy Broderick. What do you think?'

'Dustbins.'

'Yeah. Now think: Jimmy Broderick and transport.'

'I don't get it.'

'His transport?'

'Car.'

'Very good. Parked outside his house. Seldom locked.'

'Yeah. So?'

'What day is today?'

'Wednesday.'

'Temperature?'

'Low eighties.'

'Imagine three days from now. The weekend. One retired trout under the back seat of Broderick's car, stewing in the eighties. Mild stink to high heaven. Brilliant.'

'Ah, Jesus, Kevin, you wouldn't.'

'We would.'

'Come on!'

'I can still hear him shouting from the sideline. That didn't cost him a thought. This doesn't cost me a thought, either. All you need to do is keep watch. That's all. Come on, it's a brilliant idea.'

I smiled. It was. Bitter and twisted but brilliant. And Broderick deserved it.

'It's more than brilliant. It's epic.'

'Heroic.'

'Mythological.'

Kevin nodded.

'I will be a leg end in my own lifetime.'

We spent the night cycling around, waiting for darkness or dusk, at least. We did wheelies up and down the paths, we raced each other out the Dublin road, we sat on the Green bridge laughing. Kevin dangled the trout between his legs, strutting along the parapet. Two old ladies passed, he shook the fish after them when he thought they wouldn't see. We were kids again.

We spun yarns about what we'd do to Broderick. Our

laughter echoed across the fields to Mullarney. We were totally happy, up to devilment, the way we functioned best. There was nothing between us but the common aim of making Jimmy Broderick's life a misery and that was enough, that was everything.

'We should try pulling a big one on Broderick every year, right to the bitter end, right to sawing the arse out of his coffin.'

'Or digging him up and sitting him on the graveyard wall.'

Our imaginations ran riot. And then it was dark and we cycled up through the village and past Broderick's house. His car was outside. The porch light was on.

'Looks like he's expecting someone,' Kevin said.

A car passed. We cycled to the end of the road and turned.

'Just keep spinning around the road and whistle if there's a sign of anyone.'

He swerved behind Broderick's car, laying his bike on the path and trying the driver's door. It opened. He pushed the driver's seat forward and knelt in the back, allowing the door to close behind him. I circled on the road, counting. Thirty seconds, a minute, two minutes.

'Come on, come on, come on.'

Another minute. I cycled past the car. Kevin had taken the clips off the back seat; I turned and watched the road. I heard the seat clicked into place. Car lights came from the village. I cycled away. Kevin stayed put. The car passed and he was out, on his bike. We were gone.

'I just wish,' Kevin said, shaking his head slowly.

We were sitting in his kitchen, drinking tea. His father had gone to bed.

'So do I,' I said and we sat back, smiling.

'He'll think something rotten crawled up his hole and died.'

On Friday, coming home from work, I met Jimmy Broderick, driving as slowly as he always did, his solemn mouth closed tightly. I kept a straight face till he had passed and then I burst out laughing.

Kevin, I thought, you're one cruel genius.

We waited until Sunday afternoon and then we cycled down past Broderick's house again. His car had been driven into the garden. The doors and windows were open, the back seat propped against the wall. Broderick was carrying a basin of water from the house. Kevin slowed and saluted.

'Howya Jimmy.'

Broderick glanced up from the basin.

'Men!'

We cycled on.

'You stupid bastard,' Kevin spluttered. 'We got you. That the smell may linger till your balls fall off in the frosts of winter.'

'Amen,' I intoned. 'Amen.'

*

I was fast asleep, dead to the world. And then my father was shaking me.

'Tim! Tim! Wake up.'

'Yeah. What? What is it?'

'Kevin was on the phone. We better go down, he says his father beat him up.'

'Shit, right, right. I'm up.'

I rolled out of bed, pulling on a tee shirt and jeans, slipping into runners, following my father downstairs and out to the car. The headlights opened up the lane to us. I looked at the clock on the dashboard. Half past two. And then we were driving into Bracken's yard. My father was out of the car before me, pushing open the kitchen door. I saw, over his shoulder, Kevin rolled in a ball on the floor. And then my father was beside him, unlocking his fingers, easing his hands from his face. There was blood between Kevin's fingers, black blood on the crown of his head.

'Ring the doctor,' my father said.

I went into the hall and lifted the phone. Bracken was standing on the landing at the top of the stairs. He didn't move. When I'd spoken to the doctor I went back into the kitchen. My father had put a cushion under Kevin's head. I whispered to him that Bracken was upstairs.

'Leave him there. I'll talk to him later. What did the doc say?'

'He's on his way.'

My father sighed deeply, holding Kevin's hand in his own.

'You saw him earlier tonight?'

'Yes. I was here till twelve.'

'And was there any sign of this?'

I shook my head.

'There was talk about getting up to load cattle in the morning. And then his father went to bed. That was it.'

'Nothing else?'

'No.'

'Not that that makes any difference.'

He turned back to Kevin, holding his hand, whispering to him. And then there were lights in the yard. I opened the door to the doctor.

I waited outside while he examined Kevin. I didn't want to hear. My father came out to me.

'There's an ambulance on the way. He's sending him to Naas.'

'What's the story?'

'He doesn't know. Concussion maybe. A fracture maybe.'

'I'll go with him,' I said.

'Okay,' he sighed. 'I'll stay here. Talk to his father. God only knows why, but anyway . . .' He sighed again. 'Jesus, where is it going to end?'

We went back inside. I stood near the door. Kevin was moaning softly. I thought the ambulance would never come but it did, backing slowly into the yard, the blue light circling the walls of the sheds. And then we were inside. The nurse and myself sitting across from Kevin.

'I'll follow you up,' my father said. 'Once I'm finished here.'

I nodded. We drove down the lane.

'Your brother?' the nurse asked.

'Yeah,' I said, without the slightest hesitation.

I stayed with Kevin, through casualty and X-rays and down to the ward where he was kept for observation. They'd just put him to bed when my father arrived. He'd already spoken to the night sister.

'You're a tough man, looks like you came through again.'

I thought Kevin was going to cry but he swallowed hard.

'They're keeping you here till this evening. We'll collect you then. You can come and stay with us for a couple of days. Anyway, time enough for that then. Try to sleep now.'

'Thanks,' his speech was slurred.

'I'll be outside,' my father said.

When he'd left the ward, I said: 'Do you want me to stay?'

Kevin shook his head. His eyes were closed, his jaw turning a blackened green, his head wound lightly bandaged.

I kissed him on the cheek. 'Sleep well, compadre.'

I walked softly to the end of the twilit ward and saluted but his eyes were closed.

Driving home, I opened the window of the car. The day was fresh and clean, still dewy before the sun baked everything.

'He'll be okay,' my father said. 'Luckily. It could have been otherwise. He has a hairline fracture.'

'Did you talk to his father?'

'Yeah. For all the sense he made. He said Kevin went

into his room when he was going to bed, told him he wasn't loading the cattle and that he was finished getting up at all hours. He says he followed him downstairs again and that Kevin pushed him and he gave him a few thumps.'

'They must have been mighty thumps to do all that.'

'He says he banged his head off the table.'

'Very original.'

'That's what I thought. Did Kevin say anything?'

'No, not a word.'

We drove through Kilcullen. I was reminded of the morning after my mother's death, sitting at the kitchen table, just the pair of us, eating breakfast, neither of us speaking. I wondered whether my father remembered that. I was on the verge of asking him but I didn't.

We were coming into Moone when he spoke again. 'You won't credit this. When I was leaving Bracken's, Eddie followed me out to the car and leaned in the window and asked me to make sure Kevin had everything he wanted. And, you know, I think he genuinely meant it.'

I thought of Kevin in the hospital ward, alone, and his father at home, probably lying awake, alone, and I knew there was nothing I could do about it. I was eighteen years old. I couldn't get beyond now with my own father, I couldn't influence his life or mine. The only one I seemed to be able to connect with was Hannah. I felt useless, hopeless. Nothing had changed. This weight would go on for ever, pulling Kevin and his father down, pulling the rest of us with them so that we could never breathe easily, ever. That was how it felt. And the air outside, the summer day coming up in the east did nothing to relieve the claustrophobia.

It was after eleven when my father woke me. 'I rang work to say you wouldn't be in today, I told them there was a family illness. And I rang the hospital. Kevin's okay. He'll probably be out this evening. I thought maybe you'd get the bus to Naas at lunchtime and I'll collect the pair of you when I finish work.'

'Fine.'

'I better go then and do a bit.'

On the bus, I thought of how this might as easily have happened a week later. Hannah would have arrived home to see the ambulance in the yard. She didn't need that. None of us needed any of this. Let Kevin come and stay with us, for good if needs be, but there was no sense in this happening again because one of these times would be the last time. I'd told Kevin that. I'd tell him again. The only way out was to keep himself and his father apart.

He was asleep when I got to the ward. I bought a magazine and sat beside his bed. It was late in the afternoon when a nurse woke him. He didn't seem to realize I was there.

'I think you're right as rain,' she said. 'Just don't go heading any footballs for a couple of days. And you're friend is here.' She moved away.

'How's it going?' I asked.

'Fine. A bit sore.'

'Your eye is open anyway. How's the head?'

'Wobbly.'

'Did they say you could go?'

'Don't know yet.'

'My father's coming up later.'

'Okay.'

'What happened, Kev?'

He didn't answer for a long time. He seemed to be sifting through things, trying to put them together.

'You seemed all right when I was leaving.'

'Cattle. He wanted me up at four to load them. I told him I wouldn't. I did the last three loads. I went back down to the kitchen. I was going to leave, just go and sleep in the loft, so he wouldn't find me. He followed me downstairs, tore my shirt. I pushed him and then he hit me a couple of times and I fell. So he gave me a few digs while I was on the ground. Then he went back upstairs. I thought he was getting his gun but he didn't come back down. I couldn't stop the bleeding. That's when I rang you.'

It all sounded so clinical when he told it. Maybe because it was.

'It's still there. He still has it for me.'

I didn't argue with him. There was no point. We just sat quietly while visitors came and went, until my father arrived. He brought a change of clothes for Kevin.

'They're paroling you,' he said. 'Good man.'

It was a strange journey home. None of us had anything to say. We were almost into Castledermot when my father spoke.

'I'd like you to stay in our house, if you don't have any objections. It might be the best.'

'Okay,' Kevin said.

I made up the bed in the spare room. The doctor called after tea.

'You're a lucky man. Get out of that place below, stay out of it.'

On my way to bed, I went in to see Kevin.

'Will you be all right tomorrow, while I'm working?'

'Course.'

'You can stay here as long as you like, you know that. For good if you want. We can talk about it when Hannah gets back.'

'I'll see.'

'You really should stay.'

'I shouldn't have to stay.'

'Yeah, I know that Kev, we all know that. But just do it.'

'I said I'll see.'

'Goodnight.'

'Goodnight.'

I closed the door behind me, went into my room, lay on my bed. The frustration was back. There was nothing I could do. He wouldn't listen to me, he'd do what he wanted to do. If he stayed it would be because he wanted to, not because of any influence I had over him. I went back through the week. Broderick's, the enjoyment of that madness, the fun of it all, the innocence and then, without any warning, this. It frightened me and I didn't understand it.

I came straight home from work the following day, cycling hard up Mullaghcreelan, wanting to be back. There was a coldness in my stomach, an inkling that the house would be empty, that Kevin would have gone back home, that the whole thing would have come to a bitter head. I had visions of blood in the yard and broken glass on Bracken's kitchen floor. I rode harder, leaning out over the handlebars, pushing my head into the little wind there was. The closer I got to home, the more certain I was that something terrible would have happened. I could hear the silence already, the terrible quietness in our house, the open doors and empty rooms. It would be like the time after my mother had died. The stillness when I got in from school. I remembered it so well, it didn't even seem like a memory, it was something that was always there.

Turning into the lane, I skidded through the gateway, dropping my bike, pushing open the back door. The kitchen was empty. I went into the hall and called. Kevin's voice from upstairs. I was up, three steps at a time. He was lying in the bath.

'You all right?'

'Yeah. Sore. But this is good.'

I sat on the side of the bath staring at the mustard skin along his ribcage.

'It looks sore.'

'Yeah . . . well.'

I took a cloth from the shelf and washed his shoulders.

'The old bollocks rang.'

'Did you talk to him?'

'Huh.' His laugh was dismissive.

'Did he say anything?'

'Asked me how I was. That was about it.'

I finished washing him. 'I'll go and put something on for dinner. You stay there. Relax.'

'The spuds are ready. They're on the cooker.'

'Thanks.'

'Maybe, after dinner, we could get out for a while.'

'Sure. I might get the car.'

'That'd be good.'

We did go out that night. We drove through Tullow, to Rathvilly. We didn't talk too much, just enjoyed the slow drive through the evening sunshine. We stopped off and had a coffee in a pub and then we drove home again. My father was waiting for us when we got home.

'I went down to see your father,' he told Kevin. 'He said he rang today.'

'Yeah.'

'I told him I thought you should stay here a while, till things are sorted out, till we all get a chance to sit down and think about things, till you feel things are sorted in your head. I think it'd be good to wait till Hannah gets home. How do you feel about that? It's your decision. I'm not trying to sway you one way or the other.'

'No, that's okay.'

'Just take your time.'

Kevin nodded.

My father went out into the yard but he was back in a couple of minutes.

'So long as you don't think I'm trying to run the show, Kevin. It's up to you. You're not a prisoner.'

'I know that.'

'Right, right, good.'

Later, after my father had gone to bed, we laughed about that. We were in the sitting room,. listening to music.

'I think this is as bad on him as it is on you,' I said.

'Sure it is. It's not really that bad for me at all, not where it counts. See, you don't understand it, every time this happens I get harder, I get tougher, I grow away from everything he tries to do, I'm nearly clear of it all. It's the only certain way of doing it. I'm able for it, you don't understand that. No one does. But I know it, in here.'

He tapped his head.

'And what about the rest of it, the cracked ribs, the side of your face, the fractured skull?'

He dismissed it with a wave of his hand.

'I wish I could believe that,' I said, sharply.

'You don't have to. I'm the only one who has to do that.'

'And that's all that matters to you. No one else has an opinion. It must be great to be so sure.'

He said nothing.

Later, when I was half asleep, he came into my room and got into bed.

'You don't have to carry me,' he whispered.

'I'm not trying to carry you but I don't want to have to pick up the pieces either.'

'You won't.' He kissed me.

'Let me do this for you.' Gently, he took my prick in his hand. I tried to touch him.

'No, just you,' he said.

I don't remember him leaving my room that night, just his body beside me, his hand on me, easing me to sleep.

*

Sometimes, when I'm awake, in the afternoon, lying on our bed, the window open on the early autumn that doesn't yet know that summer is over, I create visions of you in my head. I close my eyes and manufacture these fantasies. In one, I imagine you lying half-asleep in the old orchard, just as you used to do, just as I saw you there three or four weeks ago. It's as recent as that. I have to keep reminding myself because some things I can no longer remember cleanly. Some things are shrouded, some are just blurred about the edges. But some things are as clear as water and always will be.

Anyway, in this waking dream, I put you lying in the orchard and your eyes are closed and a bird comes down and lights on your shoulder. I make it a robin because you pointed a robin out to me once, one that came and perched on the handle of a fork when we were working in the garden. So I allow this robin on to your shoulder. And then I lose control. The colour of your skin changes, it fades to the shade of an old Polaroid and I know you're lying dead in the grass and then the edge of the picture is blurred, the bit about your shoulder, and I know the bird has changed its shape, it has grown and I know, despite the opaqueness, that its wings are wide and dark, no longer the wings of a robin. So, I abandon the fantasy because I cannot control it any more.

And now I reassure myself. Your skin was never the colour of yellow candles. I remember the way your face flushed when we were fucking, the brightness and heat of your cheeks. The cinnamon colour of your body at this summer's end. I satisfy myself with the memory of colour. And I know that when the real dreams come you'll be there, they'll be your dreams and I'll be the spectator. They'll be the dreams of the optimist I never was. You'll be the one who shows me where things are to be found.

In the meantime, I go on looking for the reminders. I know where some of the are – the photographs, the clothes, the perfume, the grave – but I believe there are others and I keep searching for them, in the sounds around me, in the garden at dawn, on the landing at dusk. I search, even though I know the dream is the thing, the dream resurrected by your memory.

Isn't it strange that memory has become my obsession, that the past is all I have to look forward to with you?

*

When I got back from work on the Thursday of that week Kevin wasn't about. At first I thought he might have gone for a walk; there was nothing to suggest anything else. No missing clothes, he had none with him.

I was getting the dinner ready when he rang.

'I'm at home,' he said.

I said nothing.

'I came back this morning. I wanted to be back before Hannah gets here. No point in her walking in on all this shit.'

Still I said nothing.

'This gives me time to get settled in. You're annoyed.'

'No I'm not.'

'You think I'm mad.'

'I didn't say that.'

'So what's the matter?'

'Nothing, I told you. It's your business.'

'That's right, it is. But you think it's yours.'

'No I don't.'

'Course you do. I can't explain this to you. You don't understand, you can't. Come down and see me after dinner.'

'And what'll I find? Will you be alive or dead?'

'I'll be alive. I'll always be alive.' He was laughing. He meant it. 'Ten days. Exam results. Freedom. I'll be alive.'

'Did you see your father?'

'Yeah.'

'And?'

'He asked me if I was all right. End of conversation.'

'And will that satisfy him?'

'Who cares?'

'It's not just next week, Kev, it's not just the results. You have to hang around until October, until college starts, remember that.'

'I remember. And you'll come down!'

'Okay.'

I thought my father would be livid when I told him Kevin had gone but he took it well.

'I knew he wouldn't stay here. Why should he, I suppose. That's how he sees it. It's just a question of his father keeping himself under control.'

'It's a long way to October.'

'It is. When is Hannah home?'

'Saturday night.'

'Aye, well that itself, at least it won't be just the pair of them.'

Kevin's father was in the kitchen when I called that night. The two of them sitting at the table, drinking tea, the television on in the corner, it looked like any ordinary house, any ordinary family.

Kevin poured tea for me, touching the back of my neck as he leaned over. Would this be a new way of getting at his father, I wondered?

Bracken spoke to me a couple of times, about the weather and work. I mentioned Hannah's homecoming.

'The weather was every bit as good here,' he said.

'Still, I'm sure she'll have a good time.'

'Aye, no doubt. No doubt.'

Everything so ordinary.

Later, Kevin and myself walked down to the fields. We stopped to watch Hote cropping the grass in the well field.

'I can explain a hundred times but I can't really make you understand,' Kevin said. 'I won't let him break me, I won't let him tie me to this place but I won't let him feel he can dump me out of it either. I'll go when I decide. That's the best I can do.'

'I understand all that.'

I saw no point in fighting with him.

'It might be better when Hannah is here. Two of you.'

'Yeah.'

We walked on, across the field and into the next one.

'You slept well the other night,' Kevin said. 'It was nice, watching you.'

'It was nice.'

'Just give me time, will you? Give me time to surprise you.' There was an earnestness in his voice. 'Give me the next few months, till the end of the summer, till we go away. I'm not asking you to do anything more than that. It can all change when we get to Dublin, no promises, no ties, nothing beyond the end of September.'

We had stopped walking. We were standing in the middle of the field, one side of Kevin's face was greeny blue where the bruising still leafed his skin.

And then, as if he knew what I was thinking, he added: 'You have my word, if it's gone by then, it's gone. But give me the time to try, give yourself the time.' And then he laughed out loud.

'And if it doesn't work you need never touch my prick again, not even with a tweezers!'

I laughed, too. We stood there in the open field, laughing uproariously.

'Nor a forceps?'

'Nor a tongs.'

'Hayfork?'

'Nope.'

We walked back home, laughing.

*

Hannah came home that Saturday night. Her friends dropped her back just after eleven. I made sure I was in the house when she arrived.

When he heard the car in the yard, her father went out to meet her. He carried in her bags and then she was there, in the kitchen light, her skin tanned, her hair blazing, a fresh smell of life all around her.

'Welcome home,' Kevin said.

Hannah flinched when she saw his face but she said nothing.

'Welcome back,' I said.

'You had a good time?'

She turned to her father. 'Yeah, great, brilliant. It was lovely. The only way to live.'

She rooted in one of her cases and produced presents for each of us. Whiskey for her father, tee shirts for Kevin and me.

'I'll bring your cases upstairs,' Bracken said.

When he'd gone Hannah said: 'What happened to your face, Kevin?'

'He did. I'll tell you about it tomorrow. It's okay, it's all sorted. So tell us about Spain, how many guys did you shift?'

That night I lay in bed with my eyes closed and tried to recreate the sight, the smell, the brightness that had come into Bracken's with Hannah. I fell asleep thinking of her, wanting to be with her, wishing she'd come in the night, to my room and my bed.

I didn't see her or Kevin the next day, I thought it best to leave them to talk things out and she was back to work on the Monday but she came down to the house that night. My father was there when she called. He told her about what had happened.

'I wanted him to stay here, till you got back, but he wouldn't.'

'You were really good to him, both of you. Everything seems all right now but you just never know when it's going to blow up again. All we can do is wait and see.'

'That's about it,' my father said. 'Nothing else you can do.'

Walking back down the lane I asked her about Spain.

'It was good but the girls were a bit of a wash-out, I wouldn't go with them again. Predictable.'

'I'm glad you're back,' I said.

'Are you?'

She was smiling.

'Yes, I am.'

'Did you miss me?'

'Yes.'

'Looks like you hardly had time, with all the drama.'

'I had the time.'

'Well now I'm back, I'm glad I'm back. I'm glad you missed me. I missed you, too.'

'Did you?'

'Actually, I did.'

And she kissed me, standing in the lane where anyone might have seen us, where Kevin might have come on us. But I didn't care, just to touch her again, just to taste her tongue, to feel her body through her dress.

'Maybe I do love you,' she said. 'In a way.'

I laughed.

'Thanks,' she said.

'I'm happy. I'm ecstatic, that's all.'

'Are you?'

'Almost.'

And then I told her about Kevin's conversation with me the week before.

'It's all coming together,' I said. 'The exam results are out next week, you coming back, him and me, your father beating him up, all that stuff.'

'I'm not asking you to do anything.'

'It's just not that easy for me.'

'Maybe you should be a priest, conscience and all that.'

'I don't think so, Hannah.'

'Neither do I.' She kissed me again, a soft kiss.

'Just don't worry about it. There's no point in saying anything till the results come out. It's okay, you know that.'

'Is it, are you sure?'

'Yes, of course.'

'Thanks. You're great.'

'I know. Señorita Sensational.'

*

Once, you found some old records in my room, one evening when I was out somewhere, and when I came back you played a couple. We laughed about them.

'This one, listen to this one,' you said. 'I like this one.'

It was a record I'd bought the week Hannah came back from Spain, one I'd heard on the radio, an old song, heard by chance. I cycled to Carlow, got them to order it for me, played it over and over when I was going to sleep, learned the words. If anything, that was Hannah's song. Maybe you guessed there was something in it, when I croaked along with the record, word perfect after eleven years.

> *'Spanish is the loving tongue,*
> *Soft as springtime, white as spray.*
> *There was a girl I learned it from,*
> *Living down Señora way.*
> *Now I don't look much like a lover*
> *Yet I say her love words over,*
> *Late at night when I'm all alone,*
> *Mi amor, mi corazon.*

There were nights when I would ride,
She would listen for my spurs,
Fling that big door open wide,
And raise those laughing eyes of hers.
And how those hours would get to flying,
Pretty soon I'd heard her crying:
"Please don't leave me all alone,
Mi amor, mi corazon".'

'That means something to you,' you said.
'Maybe.'
'Oh, come on, don't go all coy about it. Tell me.'
'I bought it a long time ago, someone I was going out with, one of those songs.'
'More,' you said, your eyes sparkling. 'Tell me more. Who was she?'
'Hannah Bracken, she lived down the lane.'
'The woman who owns the farm?'
'Yeah.'
You laughed, then.
'Well, I hope it ended well, if we're trying to buy the field from her. I hope you did the decent thing.'
'There's more to it, I'll tell you the rest sometime.'
'You're the father of her triplets.' You were laughing.
'Not quite. Another time.'
Always another time.

*

'The exam results are out today, aren't they?' the head waiter asked.

We were serving breakfast, it was just after eight.

'Yeah.'

'What time will they be in the school?'

'About half-nine.'

'Well, get on that bike, says bollocky Bill, and get out of here at nine, go get them. Right?'

'Thanks.'

'You can remember me when you own this kip.'

'I will.'

I rang Kevin before I left the restaurant. We met at the school. Already, there were half a dozen others there. We stood about in the hall, nervously kicking the walls, watching for the office door to open.

'He collected them at half-eight,' someone said. 'He should have them written up by now.'

'Where do we open the envelopes?' Kevin asked me.

'Outside, around the bicycle sheds, away from the rest of them.'

And then the office door opened and, one by one, we went inside. The headmaster was standing by his desk. He smiled as I went in.

'Well done,' he said. 'I think you'll be satisfied.'

I winked at Kevin as I came out and went and stood in the porch. He followed me out.

'Did he say anything?' Kevin asked.

'Said he thought I'd be happy.'

'Well, let's go.'

We raced around the side of the school, across the

tarmac basketball court, down to the bicycle shed, tearing open the envelopes as we went, eyes skimming through the grades.

'Yesssssss,' I screamed. 'Yessss, yesss, yesss, yesss.'

I danced around the shed. 'We made it, we made it.'

'I didn't,' Kevin said. 'I failed.'

'What?' I felt myself go cold.

'In my bollocks,' his mouth widened into a grin. 'In my left testicular, in my right vetricular, two A's, four B's, look out Dublin, here we come, leave that Nobel prize on the table, I'll be back for it in a minute!'

We cycled to my house. I phoned my father and Kevin phoned Hannah and then I phoned the restaurant.

'Well, how'd it go?' the head waiter asked.

I told him.

'I'll be back in an hour,' I said.

'You will in your hole, says bollocky Bill. We'll cover for you. I'll see you in the morning. Have one for me.'

I told Kevin.

'The day is ours,' he said. 'The world.'

'Are you going to tell your father?'

'Am I what? Come on, come down with me.'

Bracken was in the yard. Kevin handed him the results.

He read them slowly.

'You done well,' he said. 'You done very well. Your mother would've been proud.'

He looked at the sheet again and then folded it neatly and handed it back to Kevin.

'And how did you get on, Tim?'

'Fine,' I said. 'Not as well as Kev, one B, four C's. But I'm happy.'

'Good. Good enough.'

He rooted in his trouser pocket and took out two five pound notes.

'There yis are, youse done well.' He handed us the money and shuffled away.

'Come on,' Kevin said.

'Where are we going?'

'Follow me.'

We sped through the village, across the bridge at the bottom of the street and down Mullarney Lane, ducking the alder branches that roofed the rough roadway. A couple of fields away a combine harvester was cutting the spring barley. Kevin barrelled along, avoiding the potholes, swinging in and out of the shadows, twisting and bending as he kept the bike moving.

At Mullarney bridge, we hoisted the bikes over the gate and cycled the last hundred yards to the ruined farmhouse.

Kevin threw his bike on the grass, took my hand and led me inside and up the stairs.

'A celebration,' he said. 'Where it began.'

He undid my jeans and pulled them down and knelt in front of me and took me in his mouth. I didn't try to stop him. He sucked me urgently, as though for breath, his tongue working, his hands holding me to him, sucking me till I came. And then I did it for him, hearing his breath, in short bursts, from somewhere above me, feeling the jerk of his body against my face, tasting his seed in my throat.

'I love this,' Kevin whispered, his voice deep and broken. 'I love this. I love you.'

My father brought me out for a celebration meal that night. We went to the hotel in Carlow.

'You did really great,' he said. 'I'm delighted for you, proud of you. You're a credit to us.' He paused, searching for words. 'I'm saying this for the two of us, your mother and myself. You did us proud. That's all.'

I'd like to have found something to say, I always imagined I would but nothing came.

The following morning, laying the tables for lunch in the restaurant, I had all kinds of fancy, fine-sounding phrases that I should have said to my father but by then it was too late.

Some time in the future, I told myself, some time the opportunity would come. The best I could do was thank him that evening, when I got home, tell him how much I'd enjoyed the night before.

'We'll do it again,' he said. 'We'll tick off every year's exams with another celebration. And a big one when Kildare win the championship.'

'The biggest one of all,' I said.

'And I have a little achievement of my own,' he said.

'Tell me.'

'I'm playing on the meggars team this evening. Davy Walsh, Derek Mooney, Colm Walsh, Frank Taaffe and myself. The greatest living exponents of the game!'

'Fair dues.'

'Arrah, it's only a challenge, but it'll be a bit of fun.'

'Well, keep them tight.'

'Oh, we will, we will. No better men.'

My father had only just left when Hannah arrived. She handed me an envelope and a package.

'Well done, genius.'

I opened the envelope, a congratulations card.

'Thanks a million,' I said, putting it on the mantelpiece.

'And the parcel. It's just something small.'

I tore the wrapping. It was a book on wildflowers. 'Now you won't be lost and you won't forget your roots when you get to Dublin!'

I kissed her. 'It's brilliant, thanks.'

'You're welcome.' She hesitated. 'I suppose I better get going.'

'Why?'

'I don't know. What are you doing?'

'Nothing.'

'Where's your father?'

'Gone to Foxhill, he's playing meggars.'

'Ah.'

'Stay,' I said.

'Okay. What'll we do?'

'I don't mind.'

For some reason I felt uneasy, I didn't know why. It was as if the comfort of other nights was missing. There was a tension that I didn't understand.

'We could go to bed,' Hannah said, quietly. 'If your father won't be back for a while.'

'No he won't, not for hours.'

'We could go to bed, then.'

And we did, we climbed the stairs to my room, undressed self-consciously, slid into the cool bed and held each other without saying much, just lay there, feeling the kiss of skin on skin. And then there was a knock on the kitchen door. I froze, waiting, listening. Another knock and Kevin's voice calling my name.

'Shit, the door isn't locked,' I whispered.

'So?'

'If he comes in, comes up here.'

'Let him, it's not a crime. Relax, Tim.'

And then he was gone, the sound of his bicycle tyres on the gravel, the silence.

'If it happens, it happens,' Hannah said, kissing me. 'You worry too much. I bet you've been waiting to get me in here and now you're all uptight. You have, haven't you?'

I nodded.

'And are we going to blow it?'

I giggled.

'Okay, we are going to blow it,' Hannah laughed.

We stayed in bed as long as we dared and then I walked her home.

'I'll miss you when you go away,' she said.

'You can come to Dublin at the weekends.'

'That'd be nice.'

'Maybe we'll end up in college together. Maybe you'll go back.'

'Don't get too carried away.'

It was dusk but still hot.

'Imagine if this summer went on for ever,' she said. 'Through September and October and up to Christmas. If the weather never broke. It's hard to imagine it ever being cold or wet or miserable again.'

'Now who's getting carried away?'

'I dream too,' Hannah said. 'Maybe I just tie my dreams down.'

We were at the end of the lane, just across from Bracken's yard, standing in the shadow of the trees and kissing. Over Hannah's shoulder, I saw her father cross the yard to the shed and then cross back with an armful of turf.

'Can I ask you something?'

'Sure.'

'You told me once that love fucks everything up, that's what you said.'

'Yeah.'

'But the other night, you told me you loved me.'

'Did I?'

'Yes, you did.'

'It's just different, isn't it? I'm not asking you to marry me or anything. That's what I was talking about the last time, about people trying to trap you, keep you for themselves.'

'I like having you for myself,' I said.

'Well, you have, haven't you?'

'Have I?'

'Yeah, you have. Tonight was lovely.' She looked straight into my eyes. 'It was lovely, Tim. I never let anyone come like that before, never tasted anyone. That's the truth.'

Afterwards, often afterwards, I thought about that, about what Hannah said that night, standing under the trees across from her house. It was one of the nicest, most artless things I ever heard.

And I thought about it that night, too, lying in bed. I knew it was time to talk to Kevin, to tell him I couldn't go on with him the way we'd been going. I wouldn't tell him about Hannah, time enough to think of that when I had to and, anyway, that wasn't the issue, I was doing this for myself, not for anyone else. This was just about him and me. I fell asleep with everything clear in my head, knowing what I would say and how. I prepared the answers to every argument Kevin might have.

*

Last weekend, I found a small plastic disc with your family crest embossed on it. It was part of a keyring you'd bought on a school tour years ago. It got caught in the door one evening last winter and the disc shattered. The broken pieces fell on to the gravel outside and neither of us ever bothered to pick them up. Bit by bit they disappeared under the stones. And then, last Saturday morning, I saw the coloured crest glinting in the sunshine. I knew, immediately, what it was but I left it there.

To bring it in would be to change something else and enough has been changed already, too much. But you know that. You know that all too well.

*

The following day most of my certainty had evaporated but I steeled myself to tell Kevin anyway. I'd take as much time as it took but I'd do it. I didn't ring him that evening. This had to be done face-to-face so I called to the house and we went to the back river to swim. We hadn't been there in weeks and I wanted to be well away from the lane, away from anywhere we might meet Hannah. Cycling out the Barrack road, I remembered the last time we'd been there but I put it out of my mind and planned what I wanted to say.

We swam silently in the bright water and then dressed on the bank.

'You're quiet,' I said.

'Yeah.'

'Why?'

'Dunno really.'

'Course you know. What is it?'

He laughed, a cold, short laugh.

'I thought, when the exams results came, that I was flying. I just don't feel much like that anymore. Just something in my head. I thought I'd get the exams and that'd be it, I'd be free, clear.'

He looked away from me, back along the river to where it twisted between the spears of water iris and into the Rocks. His eyes were moist.

'But it isn't like that, it isn't going to be that way, there's too much inside that there's no way of getting out. And no way of getting away from. I thought I'd won when I got the exams but the more I think about it the more I know I'll never beat him. He's in my blood.'

'It's just a reaction,' I said. It was the best I could manage. 'It'll be all right when we get out of here. College is the cure. The Shoebox Shitters find their natural home.'

But he didn't smile, no reaction whatsoever.

'Is there something happening with your father?'

'I wish there was. There doesn't have to be. It won't take him long to realize how well he's done his job, he'll nose it out and then he'll be happy.'

'No he won't.'

'Yes, he fucking will.'

'Did you talk to Hannah?'

He shook his head.

'You should.'

'Why?'

'She might be able to help.'

'It's not like you can drain it, it's not like a transfusion will get it out of my system. It's a killer.'

'Don't be stupid, Kev.'

He gathered his togs and towel from the grass. 'Let's go.'

I said nothing going home and when we got to my house Kevin just waved me in and went on down the lane alone.

213

I rang Hannah at work the next morning and told her what he'd said.

'I'm not asking you to do anything. I'm just telling you,' I said.

'I'll try to talk to him. But you know Kevin, how stubborn he can be.'

I didn't see either of them that night or the next. And then Hannah called, just after ten on the Thursday night.

'I think he's coming round,' she told me. 'We talked a bit on Tuesday and I couldn't get any good out of him but last night he was pretty okay. You know the way he is, he'll probably be setting the world on fire tomorrow. That's Kevin.'

'I'm glad.'

'And how are you?'

'Fine.'

'Where's your father?'

'I'm not sure. Out somewhere.'

'Good.'

She led me upstairs and we lay on my bed. I was uneasy, listening for the car in the yard.

'It'll be great when you can come to Dublin for weekends,' I said. 'When we won't have to worry about being disturbed. That's what I'm looking forward to.'

'How come you guys can never live for what's happening now? You're always thinking about what might happen tomorrow or next week or next year.'

'Are we?'

'Yeah, you and Kevin. If it's not what might be good it's what might go wrong. Just shut up about it and kiss me or I won't visit you at all.'

Walking Hannah home that night, I said: 'Isnt it strange how we lived so close for so long and never really noticed each other much?'

'If it's not the future it's the past,' she laughed. 'Try and stay in the here and now, you're a frigging time traveller, Tim.'

On nights like that, when there was just Hannah and me, I almost forgot Kevin or, at least, that part of Kevin that impinged on the piece of my life that was Hannah. Looking back, I'm not sure whether things were more or less clear then, whether it's easier to compartmentalize in the selfishness of youth or whether distance clarifies. I do know that on those nights I could think of no one other than Hannah and I know that I was intent on making space for her in my life, even if it meant rearranging the space that Kevin had. Like Hannah said, Kevin was changeable, he'd be up again the next day and I'd talk to him then because I couldn't go on like this, hiding sister from brother. And what hope was there for me in Dublin if Hannah couldn't be around just because Kevin was there? None.

But life didn't allow for that. Every time I saw Hannah my heart raced. Every time I lay down with her or touched her or kissed her I was lost. And it wasn't just the excitement of the unknown, the kind of excitement I'd felt with Kevin when we first kissed. This was something altogether different. And on that night I knew there was no time left.

I called for Kevin the following afternoon.

'How are you feeling?'

'I'm okay,' he said. 'Better.'

'Good. Let's walk.'

We went down the river road and sat on one of the benches, across the river from Mullarney. A couple of kids were playing in the shallows near the bridge. 'I want you to listen to me,' I said. 'Just hear me out, okay?'

'Yeah, all right.'

'I've been thinking a lot about us, Kev. About the last few months. I don't see any point in going on with it. I think it's better if we got back to where we were. I'm not saying there was anything wrong. I enjoyed it but there's no future in it for me, it's just going to get in the way. Like you said, I'm not a real queer.'

I saw that he was about to speak but I didn't give him the chance.

'I know what you're going to say, that you gave me time to make up my mind, but I don't need that time, Kev. I've made it up. That's why I'm telling you now because I know and I want you to know, so we can get on with things. With making Jimmy Broderick's life a misery.'

I tried to make light of it but he didn't laugh.

'Why?' he asked.

'Because I know. I enjoyed what we did but it's not easy for me, it's just sex, it's not love. The love I have for you

216

goes back all the way to when we were kids. It's a different kind of love. The sex isn't part of it. I wanted to try it and I enjoyed it but that's all there was to it.'

'No future.'

'No,' I said, very quietly. 'No future. For that part of it. But there is for us, same future we always had.'

'I asked you not to decide until . . .'

'But I know, Kev, I know what I feel,' I interrupted. 'I had to tell you, to get back to the way things were. That's all. This gives us both a chance, when we get to Dublin, we're clear of that part. You'll find someone there.'

'And there's nothing else, no one else?'

'No, Kev. It's just between me and you. I'm sorry.'

He got up and walked away, I followed him. Over the bridge, up to the Cuckoo steps, across the fields to Mullarney. He stopped then. 'Why are you following me?'

'Why not? I always followed you.'

'I suppose,' he said. 'Why not? And why not once for old times' sake?'

'Okay.' I was relieved that I'd said what I said.

We went into the ruined house and up the stairs. I masturbated him and then he masturbated me. And that was that. I don't know what Kevin was thinking of but my mind was blank. I didn't think of the day on the bog or the night in my bed or the afternoon in his loft when the motes swirled and fell in the sunlight while we talked. I thought of none of that. I just got it over with, watched his hand on my prick, saw his seed scatter on the ground. That was all and it was done.

'Here it began and here it ends,' Kevin said. He sounded like a priest intoning a prayer. 'This is the sacred house. I don't think we should ever come back here. It served its purpose.'

I nodded. Kevin stepped outside and I scuffed our come into the ground.

'Isn't it odd,' he said, afterwards, 'the way people can get to you even when they're not around, how they can change your life without even being there.'

I didn't ask him to explain. I thought I knew what he meant and, anyway, I felt free then and that was all that really mattered. I had done everything that had been asked of me, I'd been part of what he'd gone through over the summer months and now I wanted to be part of something else. I told myself we could get back to the way we had been, it would take a little time but nothing was beyond redemption.

I was free, I was happy, I was in love.

*

Yesterday, walking through the hall, I heard a voice, from upstairs. A voice whispering softly. I stopped in a scarf of sunlight from the open door. My skin goosebumped, shivering in the dead heat of the late afternoon. I couldn't hear what the voice was saying, couldn't separate one word from another, but I knew it was yours. I stood at the foot of the stairs, petrified and elated. And slowly I climbed those steps, pausing on each, listening, feeling the heat trickle from my back as I stepped into the shade at the end of the stairway. Sometimes the whisper came, sometimes there was silence and I'd wait until it began again, moving on then, step by step, to the landing at the top. And I stopped there, too, aching for one distinctive word, afraid of what you might be saying. So many things in my head. I wanted to see you and, yet, I was afraid of how you'd look. How much or how little could you have changed in less than a month? I thought back to the evening in the morgue. How beautiful you were, how much the same as you'd been the last time I saw you alive, yet how completely transformed. No light, no life, no voice.

But now your voice had come back for me.

Moving along the landing, the air trembling with the sound from the room, I knew I'd been right, you had been out there in the orchard. You came back there and now you were here, in my room, our room, whispering, the way you whispered at night in bed, even though the house was empty.

'I like whispering in bed,' you told me. 'It makes everything we say important.'

And now you'd come back to resume that intimacy. I wanted you but I was afraid of who you were, I knew you wouldn't be the same, couldn't be. Out there, wherever it was, things were different from here.

The whispering stopped. I was at the half-open door, absolutely still, sweat streaming down my face. I could smell hope and fear all around me. I wanted to push the door open, feel the sun and the air coming through the

*open window, see you, hear you, feel your touch, I didn't
care how cold or how different that touch might be. Just
to feel you there. Just that.*

*The whispering again. My hand on the door, palm flat
against the wood, pushing it open, the sun in my face, the
whispering voice, your voice. You. Here. The room empty
but the whisper going on, still there. I stepped inside,
already knowing the sound, knowing where the voice came
from. And I began to cry, not quietly but with great,
breathless gulps, sucking in the air that wouldn't come,
retching. I sat on our bed, my head down, trying to calm
myself, trying to find normality. Easing myself back from
the brink of despair that comes with hope in a hopeless
situation, lying back on the bed, closing my eyes, letting
the sun wash my face, hearing the whisper above me, water
in the attic tank, mumbling as it's mumbled for years.*

*And then I fell asleep and when I woke it was almost
dark and the whispering had stopped.*

*

It was a strange weekend, the second last in August. On
the Friday night Kevin and myself went to the pictures in
Carlow. We hitched in and out. It was a good night, we
laughed a lot. We planned fresh torments for Jimmy
Broderick. Kevin was in fine form, composing his songs
while we waited for a lift.

> 'Poor old Jimmy Broderick,
> He is nothing but a prick,

Found a fish in the back of his car,
"Now," he says, "you've gone too far."
Cannot keep his old man hard,
Runs frustrated round the yard,
Tries to screw his wife, she shouts:
"Off you go and ride the trout."
- He takes the fish into the garden,
Waits for his langer to semi-harden
But, when he finishes the screw,
Trout says: "Jimmy, I've had better eels than you."'

'Good one,' I said.

'But not up to my usual scathing standard. It needs work. Wouldn't it be great to write a whole dose of songs about wankers, real wankers that we've known.'

We passed an hour composing titles. It was a good night.

'What are you doing tomorrow night?' Kevin asked, when he was leaving.

'Don't know,' I said. 'I'm on a wedding. It might go on late.'

'You don't want to go somewhere then?'

I shook my head. 'I'd say I'll be knackered. I'll see you on Sunday.'

My father let me have the car that Saturday night. I got home just after five and Hannah called at a quarter past seven. We drove to the pictures in Carlow. The same film I'd seen the night before.

Hannah laughed when I told her. 'We could have gone somewhere else.'

'No, it was good. You liked it, didn't you?'

221

'Yeah.'

We went for coffee afterwards. I told her what I'd said to Kevin.

'Just so long as you don't think I was pushing you,' she said.

'You weren't pushing me but I couldn't go on the way things were going.'

'That's okay then. I didn't mind, you know.'

That angered me. 'Feck's sake, Hannah, how can you say that? If we're going out, we're going out. I'm hardly going to keep on with Kevin, too.'

'Fine. Just so long as you don't think it was my doing.'

'But I'd want you to push me. I'd expect it.'

'Why?'

'You're joking?'

But she wasn't. 'That's that, this is us.'

'But, if you're in love with someone, you don't want them screwing someone else.'

'And it doesn't mean you tie them up, either.'

'That's bollocks, Hannah. I'd hardly be thrilled if you were having it off with someone else.'

'And I'm not, but it wouldn't be your business.'

'Of course it would.' I couldn't believe what I was hearing.

'No it wouldn't. You went to the pictures with Kevin last night. I don't mind about that.'

'And if I screwed him afterwards?'

'It has nothing to do with me. It's not like we're married

or anything. Even if we were, you can't force people to be faithful. They decide for themselves.'

'Well, it doesn't work that way for me,' I said.

'Maybe you're too possessive.'

'Call it that if you want.'

'Okay,' she shrugged, 'we'll call it that.'

We hardly spoke on the way home. I stopped the car at my house.

'I'll walk you down,' I said.

'You won't even drive down to the house? Kevin's not going to come out checking to see who I'm with, you know.'

'Well, I'd rather not, I didn't tell him we were going out.'

She said nothing.

'Maybe I should have, maybe you think I should have rubbed his nose in it.'

'Grow up, Tim. I didn't ask you to tell him but you can't spend your life hiding it from him, either.'

'Maybe we won't have to, now. Maybe there's nothing to tell him.'

'That's up to you,' Hannah said, walking away from me.

'Fucker,' I muttered but I didn't know whether I meant Hannah or myself.

On Sunday morning I sat with my father in the church. Below us, in the main aisle, Hannah and Kevin sat together. The priest droned on. I thought about love and anger. I loved Hannah and I hated her. I wanted her and I knew I might never have her again. Whatever I'd done, I'd done for her. It would have happened in the end but it happened as it did because of her and she didn't seem to care. I didn't want a take-it-or-leave-it affair. I wanted her the way she was when she wanted me, wanted to be loved the way I loved, the way she was the night we'd talked about my mother.

Coming out of the porch, we met Kevin and Hannah.

'How's things?' I asked.

I was afraid my father might say something about the night before but he wandered away, talking to someone else.

Hannah nodded.

'All right,' Kevin sighed.

'You not in good form?'

He shrugged.

'Do you want me to call down after dinner?'

'If you want.'

'I will then. See you later.'

I followed my father to the car.

When I called, Hannah was sitting outside the back door, reading.

'Hi.'

'Kevin's in the kitchen,' she said and went back to her book.

We spent the afternoon in the house. Kevin didn't talk a lot and I didn't have much to say. I didn't feel up to nursing him back to good humour. So, there we sat. Kevin and me in the kitchen, Hannah outside the door, their father God knows where, each of us locked up by the other.

Late in the afternoon, Hannah came in and made tea and took it outside.

'Do you want to go for a cycle?' I asked.

Kevin shook his head.

'What's bugging you? Am I bugging you, did I do something?'

Another shake of the head.

'I want to get out,' I said. 'If you want to come you're welcome.'

'It's okay. You go ahead.'

I went outside and took my bike from the gable wall and cycled away, speeding up the lane, never looking back, going as fast as I could, out on to the road, down through the village, out the Athy road, through Hallahoise and down Mullaghcreelan Hill, face into the wind, hair blown back, feeling the air and the sun and the rush of release at being away on my own. I went on cycling, as hard as I could, covering the miles, feeling the sweat build up on my back, pushing it out of my eyes, going just to be gone, away from all of it, letting the afternoon tear everything from my mind. For those hours there was nobody else in my life and I didn't want anybody. My head was empty and I enjoyed the lightness that came with it.

I saw Kevin the following morning. I had a day off because I'd worked the Saturday. He was on the tractor,

coming down the lane, and I was coming from Castledermot with the paper. He pulled in and climbed down from
the cab.

'How're you feeling today?'

'I'm okay,' he said. 'Sorry about yesterday. Where did
you go?'

'Just cycling. To Stradbally and back. It was good.'

'It wasn't your fault, yesterday, it's just the way I was
feeling.'

'That's all right then. I just thought it might be.'

'No.'

'Good.'

'Listen, I better go on. I told Joe Prine I'd be up to him
before eleven, his tractor is banjaxed. I'll see you later, maybe.'

He swung back into the cab. I waved and then I went
inside and sat at the table, the paper open in front of me,
thinking about Hannah.

I saw her that evening. I waited at the top of the lane
until the factory bus dropped her.

'I'm sorry about Saturday,' I said. 'I'm really sorry.'

She shrugged.

'I just, you know . . .'

'No, I don't.'

'I just don't want things to get lost between us. Oh,
fuck, I can't explain this. I just don't understand how one
minute you can be asking me to go to bed and the next
you tell me you don't mind if I'm screwing your brother.'

'That's not what I said. I said I wasn't putting any
pressure on you to change anything for me.'

'But I want to change things for you, I want you to put pressure on me, that's part of loving someone, isn't it?'

'Maybe it is. And the next part is wanting them to change. And then the next part is blaming one another for the changes you made. I don't want that, Tim.'

We were still standing at the top of the lane. A woman passed and we were silent, waiting till she was out of earshot.

'So what do you want me to do?'

'I don't want you to do anything. Just be the way you want to be. And I will, too. The way things have been.'

'And how will I know when it's over?'

Hannah put her head to one side. 'Why is it always about the mights and maybes? It's now, Tim, it's August, nineteen eighty-four. Can we be satisfied with that?'

'I'll try,' I nodded.

'Now, I better go and get my dinner.'

'I'll give you a bar,' I said.

Hannah sat on the crossbar and we zig-zagged down the lane. She started whistling 'Raindrops Keep Falling On My Head' while we careered between the ditches, the dog roses brushing our heads. I could taste her hair in my face. I still remember that.

'See how simple things can be?' she said, when I dropped her in the yard.

'I do.'

'I'll talk to you later, will you be at home?'

'I will.'

'Are you saving up your words?'

'I am.'

And I cycled away, laughing.

*

The afternoon of your burial, when I came back from your parents' house, I went into the front porch, to open the windows. The house had been locked up for days. I closed all the windows the morning after you died. I didn't think about it, just did it as I was leaving for the hospital. Maybe, subconsciously, I thought, if everything was locked and bolted, I could keep something of you here. The same way I thought later that I could entice you back inside if I left the doors and windows open.

Anyway, that afternoon, I came back here and threw out the food that had gone stale in the kitchen and then I went upstairs and looked at the clothes you'd dropped on the floor of the bedroom. Shorts, a tee shirt, a small multicoloured scarf you'd had in your hair three days earlier. I left them where you'd dropped them.

I lay on the bed and smothered my face in your pillow. After a while, I got up and opened the bedroom window and then I went around the house, opening all the windows. Upstairs first and then down.

When I got to the front porch, there was a butterfly dead on the shelf where the plants were potted. One dead butterfly, a Red Admiral, and, nearby, the wing of another. Just that, no body, no other wings. I left them there, too. They're still there, skeletal wings in the sunshine.

*

I was in my room, listening to records, when Kevin came in.

'Your father said you were here.'

'How's it going?'

'All right. What's that?'

'It's called "Spanish Is the Loving Tongue".'

'Sounds crap. Sounds like something the Shoebox Shitters might sing. Have you anything better?' He took a handful of records from the floor.

'I passed the school today, it won't be long now, the return to the smell of polished corridors and nervous first years. Five days and they're back. But not huzzz, no sir, not huzzz, we're out of it. No more bells and bollocking from little Hitlers. No more!'

'I'm glad it makes you feel so good.'

'Ah, but it doesn't,' he said very quietly. 'It doesn't at all. It's a front.'

'Well it's a good one. You seem happy enough to me.'

'But I'm not.'

'Well, I'm convinced,' I said, lying back on the bed.

Suddenly, Kevin was leaning over me, his face a couple of inches from mine. 'It's not like that. It doesn't come that easy.'

'What are you talking about Kev?'

'About happiness. It doesn't turn on and off.'

'But things are okay, we're doing okay.'

'Only on the surface.'

'I haven't a fucking clue what you're talking about,' I said.

'I know that.'

'Well, explain it to me.'

He stood up and crossed to the record player, lifting the needle, putting it back to the beginning of the song.

'It's like I said before, it's there, there's no escape from it, there's no way out of the old bastard's web.'

'Ah, come on, Kevin, the more you think about it, the worse it gets. Don't start it. When you're down you're down and when things are okay you want them to be down again. Aren't you okay?'

I was in no humour for Kevin's mood swings. He'd come in full of the joys of life and now, it seemed to me, he was trying to pull himself down again.

'Am I?'

'Yes, you are. We all are. Do you want to do something, go somewhere?'

He was silent.

'Do you? I'm asking you.'

'It's not like that. It's never right, I never get there, I never get to it.'

'Don't understand,' I said, getting up from the bed and starting to tidy my records.

'Even the good days aren't that good. I know how good it could be but I know he's there, waiting, he'll always be there.'

'Not if you don't think about him.'

'It's not that easy.'

'I think it is.'

He was silent again.

'Let's get out of here,' I said, when I'd finished tidying.

I turned off the record player and went downstairs; Kevin followed. We walked out into the lane.

'It's like wanting and getting,' Kevin said. 'I could buy a Spandau record and like it, I could get the money together and go to their concert but it wouldn't mean I could ever write a song like Gary Kemp. See, it's wanting and getting. There's no connection.'

I laughed out loud. 'I haven't a clue what you're talking about, Kev. Is it about me and you, wanting me and you to be together?'

He shook his head. 'It's about being able to be happy, to get my head clear of him. To shake him out of my skull. You and me was only a part of it, like an anaesthetic, but I always wake up and he's here.'

'I'm telling you,' I said. 'When you stop thinking about him, he'll disappear of his own accord. But you have to give it time.'

We met Hannah at the turn of the lane. 'Where are you guys headed?'

'Nowhere in particular,' I said. 'Do you want to join us?'

She fell in beside us and we walked back the way we'd come. At the head of the lane, outside my house, Kevin stopped.

'I think I'll head home,' he said.

'Oh, come on, Kev, let's do a round of the river road and then come back here for coffee.'

'No, I'm going home.'

He turned and walked away. I let him go twenty yards and then I ran after him.

'Come on, Kev, it'll be a bit of laugh.'

'I just don't want to, okay,' his voice was quiet. 'No big deal or anything, honest to God. I just don't want to, I'm knackered.'

'Okay. I'll see you tomorrow.'

He nodded, waved to Hannah, and walked away.

'I just thought I'd try,' I said when I got back.

Hannah was doing some dance steps on the road. 'Sure.'

We walked down the street and turned onto the river road, passing other couples walking in the evening sunshine. At the end of the Green we crossed the bridge and went up Crop Hill.

'Where are we going?' Hannah asked.

'I don't mind. Dairy Lane, Mullarney, back home?'

'Choices, choices.'

'Mullarney?'

'Fine.'

We climbed the Cuckoo steps and crossed the fields. Hannah stopped and kissed me.

'What kind of flat are you going to get in Dublin?'

'Don't know. I'll have to go and look in the next week or two. What would you like?'

'Something with a balcony.'

'Of course, I should have known.'

'Looking out over the sea.'

'No problem.'

'With a big bed and white walls.'

'Spain is going to your head.'

'Why don't you come to Spain next Summer?'

'Because I'll be working myself to the bone to get my fees together. If I'm not stuck repeating.'

'You could get a week off.'

'Now who's living in the future?'

Hannah pushed me and ran, disappearing through a gap in the ditch. I chased after her, jumping through the same gap, shouting: 'I'm everybody's sex machine.'

I landed face-to-face with three women from Castledermot, their hands full of wildflowers.

'Hello Tim,' one of them said.

'Mrs Broderick.'

I glanced past them; Hannah was standing halfway across the field, laughing.

'It's a grand evening, thanks be to God.'

'Grand.'

'Mullarney is a great spot for wildflowers.'

'Great.'

'And your father is keeping well?'

'Well, ah, yeah, very well.'

'Right so, sure we'll carry on then.'

'Right.'

I sidled away, trying to walk with some dignity. When I reached Hannah, she swayed her hips provocatively.

'Ahhhh,' she said, her voice dropping an octave, 'you're so good, such a sex machine.'

'Shut up.'

'I think Maureen Broderick had an orgasm on the spot.'

'Keep walking.'

'Yes, master, yes, yes, yes,' Hannah panted. 'Whatever you say, master.'

I waited till we were through the next ditch before I grabbed Hannah and hugged her. She was still laughing.

'Shut up, they'll hear you.'

'You really picked them.'

'Who were the other two? I didn't have the neck to look at them.'

'Mrs Ledwith and Mrs Padgham.'

'Oh bollocks.'

Hannah collapsed on the grass, I flopped down beside her.

'You should have seen yourself,' she said. 'Flying through the air, roaring, "I'm everybody's sex machine". I don't know whether the three of them thought they were in heaven or hell. And then you went and disappointed them.'

'I was saving myself for you.'

'Promises, promises,' Hannah said.

I kissed her neck and the arc of her breast.

'Mmmm. Maybe you were.'

I opened the buttons of her shirt.

'Fuck,' she said quietly, 'there's someone coming along the ditch.'

We got to our feet and crossed the field.

'I know where we can go.'

I led her to the house Kevin and myself had used. We picked our way carefully up the rotten stairs, to the upstairs room. I told her about Kevin's attempts to get me to jump from the window. She laughed.

'I'm glad you didn't do it.'

I pulled off my shirt and laid it on the dusty floor and then Hannah pulled off hers. Slipping out of our jeans, we lay on the shirts, our heads close to the broken window frame.

'I think you'd like Spain.'

'I think I would, too.'

We kissed and she eased me into her.

'We have to do something about this,' Hannah whispered. 'We can't go on taking chances, 'specially not during weekends in Dublin.'

'I'll be careful,' I said.

'Or Spain.'

She rolled me over, pushing herself against me. The timber of the floor was warm under my back. Hannah raised herself, squatting on me, eyes closed, moaning loudly, not caring if anyone heard her, sweat on her face, coming suddenly, her nails digging into my shoulders, rocking backwards and forwards and easing away from me, sliding down to take my come in her hand, trailing it across my belly.

We lay that way for a long time.

'I like this room. We should come back here. I never played here.'

'You didn't qualify for cowboys.'

'But now I do. Now I can ride.'

I smiled.

'Did you come here with Kevin?'

'A few times.'

'Up here?'

I nodded. 'It was just . . . it doesn't matter. This is your room now. This is love.'

We listened to the birds in the roof above us and to footsteps, soft on the grass outside, but they passed.

'We should have done this in the field,' Hannah said, 'for Maureen Broderick. For the three of them.'

'Let's do it for them now, here.'

After we'd made love again we lay exhausted on the floor.

'I wish it was dark,' Hannah said. 'I'd love to curl up here and sleep.'

I saw Kevin a few times that week, mostly at his house when I called down. Once he came up to see me. I was listening to "Spanish Is the Loving Tongue" again but he didn't seem to notice.

'Did you do anything about looking for a flat in Dublin?'

He shook his head.

'You'll probably stay with your aunt.'

He shrugged.

'Tomorrow's the fifth of September, time to get moving. I think I'll go up next week, start sussing things out.'

He didn't respond and I was relieved. I'd assumed he'd

go into digs at his aunt's house but there was always the possibility that he'd want to share a flat with me.

'Want to go for a swim? There can't be too many days like this left.'

'I don't think so.'

'It'll be better when we get to Dublin, so many new and exciting young men,' I slipped into a poor imitation of his American twang. 'Testosterone on tap, just for you.' He grinned.

'Bulging biceps,' I encouraged. 'Long langer us days with queers from Drumineer, gays from Galway, poofs from Maynooth.'

'And the rhyming scheme collapses.'

'I tried. So are you coming for a swim?'

'No.'

When he'd left I rang Hannah and we went to the back river together. The water was still warm but autumn had started to rust the leaves along the banks. We stripped and jumped in. Hannah swam a few lengths and lay back, floating in the dusk.

'In Spain the water's hot, even late at night.'

'And Spanish is the loving tongue.'

'What?'

'Spanish is the loving tongue, soft as springtime, white as spray.'

'What's that mean?'

'It's a song.'

'Sing it for me.'

'I can't sing.'

'Say it for me.'

I rolled on my back and we floated a couple of yards apart.

'Spanish is the loving tongue, soft as springtime, white as spray, there was a girl I learned it from, living down Señora way. Now I don't look much like a lover, but I sing her love words over, late at night when I'm all alone, mi amor, mi corazon.' The words came in a babble, one line rolling into the next.

'Slow down,' Hannah said and her voice was so quiet that I did.

'There were nights when I would ride, she would listen for my spurs, fling that big door open wide and raise those laughing eyes of hers.'

'Is that it?'

'That's all I remember.'

'You're lying.'

'I'm not. I'll play it for you when I get home.'

'Is it an old song?'

'I think so. It's your song.'

We stood in the sandy river and kissed, the water around our waists, the light slipping away with the flow.

'And yet I've always sort of missed her, since that first night I kissed her,' I whispered.

Kevin phoned on the following Friday night. 'You 'round tomorrow?'

'No,' I said, 'I've a wedding. It's my last Saturday. I told

them I'd do it. Could be late. I'm here now, do you want
to come down?'

'No. I'll see you Sunday.'

'Sure.'

Hannah rang later that night. We arranged to meet
when I got home from work on the Saturday night.

'Well, that's that, says bollocky Bill,' the head waiter
said. 'Probably the last wedding of your life. If you have
sense and extract the old man in time on all occasions.'

We were standing at the back door of the hotel kitchen.

'It's been a pleasure working with you. You know
everything there is to know about the essentials of the
waiting trade, apart from boning a fish, you still make a
bollocks of that, but I'm sure you'll survive.'

'I'll be in on Tuesday,' I reminded him.

'I know that but this seems an appropriate time to say a
few well chosen words, from master to apprentice, says
bollocky Bill. And if you're stuck for employment next
summer, give us a shout. Still, you'll probably be moving
on to the building sites of west London by then.'

'Maybe not. Thanks for the offer.'

'What would keep you here, other than a pair of pert
mammaries? I'm telling you, get out early, before the rain
comes. If it rains inside you're fucked, says bollocky Bill.
So's she,' he laughed. 'Now, off with you. I'll see you
Tuesday morning.'

When I got home, my father was washing the car.

'Sure way to bring rain,' he said. 'By the way, Hannah

called in. She had to go to Carlow with her father. She said she'll see you about eight.'

'Thanks. I'll put the kettle on.'

As we ate, my father talked about going to Dublin to look for a flat.

'Maybe Friday,' he said. 'You finish up work on Thursday, don't you?'

'Yeah.'

'Will we settle on Friday then?'

'Sure.'

'What's Kevin doing?'

'Staying with his aunt, I think.'

My father nodded and drank some tea.

'Hannah's a nice girl. She's wasted in that factory.'

'I think she has plans to get out of it,' I said. 'She's brilliant at botany, there's nothing she doesn't know about flowers and stuff.'

'Maybe someone should encourage her then,' he grinned.

Hannah laughed when I told her what my father had said.

'See, all men are the same. Always planning ahead, schemers.'

But I knew she was pleased.

We were standing at the top of the lane.

'Where to?'

'I know,' I said. 'It'll be dark in an hour. Come on. You said you wanted to sleep in the room in Mullarney. Let's do it.'

It was dark inside the house and we climbed the stairs carefully. The upstairs room had the comforting smell of day's end. We undressed quickly and sat at the window, looking across the fields to where the village was a glow on the sky. Neither of us spoke, just sat touching, kissing, letting the darkness harden about us until, finally, we lay back on the floor.

'You can do it tonight,' Hannah said. 'It's okay, you can come inside me.'

'Are you sure?'

'Do I want to be a grandmother at thirty-seven?'

We fucked slowly, I wanted this to be special. I didn't want to come until Hannah came and, when she did, I pulled her on top of me and held her there, tight about me, until I came in her.

'I can feel you inside me,' she said.

We lay together, dozing, a hint of breeze through the broken window. And then there were footsteps on the stairs. I scrabbled for my jeans. Hannah was aready on her feet, not bothering with clothes. A beam from a flashlight froze me where I knelt.

'What the fuck are you doing, Kevin?' Hannah shouted.

'Did you have to screw everywhere we went?' Kevin's voice from behind the light.

'What are you talking about?'

'Ask him. I'm talking to him. You fucking cunt,' his voice was sharp as broken slate and then he was gone, clattering down the stairs and the room was blacker than hell.

'Pervert,' Hannah said. 'The vicious prick. What's he on about?'

'I told you, we were here.'

'Yeah, so? Half the village probably screwed here.'

She knelt beside me. 'He's not going to run my life. He can try it on with you, it won't work with me. It's bloody blackmail. If he'd got here earlier he might have seen something worth seeing. First Maureen Broderick, now Kevin, who the hell else wants to watch?'

We lay on our bellies, looking through the window.

'By Christ, wait till I get home, I'll give him one good bollocking.'

'I'm sure you will,' I laughed.

We stayed in the house till well past midnight. We made love again. In a way, I was glad that Kevin had found us. I knew he was angry but I knew, too, that Hannah was right. We weren't the only ones to use this house. I just wished it had been somewhere else.

'He must have followed us,' Hannah said. 'Have you guys got no imagination?'

We were walking down the lane.

'Seems not.'

'I'll ring his bloody neck.'

We reached Bracken's yard.

'Do you want to come in?'

'I better not,' I said. 'There's no point in rubbing it in. I'll come down in the morning.'

We kissed.

'I love you,' I said.

'I love you, too.'

I was halfway back along the lane when I saw a figure in a gateway.

'Kevin!'

'It's okay, you can come inside me.'

'What?'

'If he'd got here earlier maybe he'd have seen something worth seeing.'

'Maybe if you weren't sneaking around after me you wouldn't have heard any of this.'

'I heard it, I heard it all, you cunt. You. You brought her there.'

'We just ended up there,' I said.

'You lying bastard. What about the last time?'

'What are you talking about?'

'The last time, cunt. Will I remind you? This is our room, now. That's what you said, I heard you. This is love. You didn't qualify for cowboys. It was just, it doesn't matter,' his voice sing-songing my words. 'Course it doesn't matter. It doesn't matter to you.' He came out of the gateway, towards me. I tightened my fists to defend myself but he stopped a yard from where I stood.

'None of it mattered. You brought her there. That was our place. Not yours or hers. Ours. That meant something to me, fuckface. I told you that but you were too busy to listen, weren't you? Even if it was nothing but a quick wank to you it was a lot more to me but you wouldn't know that. You've only known me eighteen fucking years.'

'Bullshit.'

'Wow! Bullshit! Is that the best you can do, is your vocabulary that limited? What about your fucking Spanish love song in the river? What about that, boy?'

'You followed us.'

'I followed you everywhere, always will, you bastard. You and her. Miss come-inside-me and Mister fanny-fucker.'

'You had no right, Kevin.'

He laughed. 'No right,' he pushed his index finger into my chest, jabbing home every syllable. 'No right. No right to fuck around with someone's life. What I said, I meant.'

'Lay off,' I brushed his hand aside.

'What I said about that house, I meant, that was a sacred place. You had no right to do what you did. It's a wonder you didn't bring her out to the bog or did you just not get around to it yet?' he was crying now. 'I didn't expect any of it to last, I know better than that but you can't walk over people's hearts. He couldn't break me but you did, you fucking, fucking . . .'

His voice died. I saw him draw back his hand and I closed my eyes and waited for him to slap my face. I wanted him to do it but, instead, I heard the sound of his feet running away, up the dark lane, towards the village. I took out after him but he was gone, lost in the darkness.

Hannah rang me at lunchtime the next day. I told her about the previous night's encounter.

'He didn't show his face back here.'

'Where is he, then?'

'God knows, hiding somewhere. What's new?'

'He was genuinely upset.'

'I'm genuinely upset. Wait till I get my hands on him.'

I went down to Bracken's that afternoon. All the way along the lane, I rehearsed what I might say to Kevin. I just hoped Hannah would give me time to talk to him, without interfering.

'He's not back,' she said. 'I didn't think he would be. He'll surface tomorrow, when I'm at work.'

'What does your father say?'

'Nothing. But that's hardly surprising, is it?'

I waited until lunchtime on the Monday before I went down again. At least, I thought, I'd have time on my own with Kevin.

Bracken was in the kitchen, drinking tea.

'Good man,' he said. 'Bejasus that's one hot day, you'd think it was July, not September.'

'Is Kevin about?'

He shook his head.

'Will he be back soon?'

'Your guess is as good as mine. Never laid an eye on him yesterday nor the day.'

He drank another mouthful of tea.

'Will you tell him to give me a shout, when he gets back?'

He nodded.

I rang Hannah that night. Kevin still hadn't appeared.

'He's rubbing it in,' she said. 'He's afraid to face me.'

'You're sure?'

'Tim, you know him as well as me.'

'He's never been gone two days.'

'He's bigger now, bigger the boy the bigger the sulk. I'll ring you when he gets back, I promise. It'll be tonight or tomorrow. You're back to work tomorrow, aren't you?'

'Yeah.'

'I'll come down tomorrow night. Okay?'

'Yeah.'

I checked that my father wasn't within hearing distance.

'I love you,' I said quietly.

'Me too.'

Kevin didn't come back that night or the next. On the Wednesday his father reported him missing. Hannah rang her aunt in Dublin but he wasn't there.

'Had he a falling out with your father?' my father asked Hannah.

'No.'

'Why would he take off, sure he's only three weeks from going off to university?'

'I don't know,' she said.

I said nothing.

I finished work in the hotel on the Thursday.

'I hear there's a young fellow missing in there,' the head waiter said.

'Yeah.'

'Do you know him?'

'He lives on our lane. He's a friend of mine.'

'Well, I hope he turns up all right, says bollocky Bill.' He shook my hand.

'Good luck to you, maybe we'll see you soon.'

'Thanks,' I said.

I cycled down the avenue for the last time that summer, out on to the Castledermot road. I stopped off at Mullaghcreelan Wood and walked to the top of the hill, half-expecting Kevin to appear through the trees, half-afraid that he might.

On the Friday, I went to Dublin with my father. We looked at some flats but our hearts weren't in it.

'Maybe next week,' he said. 'We'll try again next week.'

Coming through Naas, he said: 'The last time we drove from here, Kevin was with us. I wish to God he'd phone you, just to let everyone know.'

'So do I.'

'And none of you saw this coming?'

'No.'

'He seemed in grand form the last few times he called down.'

'Yeah.'

That night we heard Kevin's name on the news, followed by the usual phrases. Hannah and her father called later that night. We sat in the kitchen, the four of us. I couldn't remember the last time Bracken had been in our house.

'He'll turn up,' Hannah said.

Her father said nothing.

The following morning, I went down to see her. 'Do you still think he's going to come back?' I asked.

'Who knows, now? He's a selfish git, you think he'd ring. He's determined to make everyone suffer as long as he can.'

'You don't think he'd have done anything else?'

'Not a chance. Life's too full of potential pain for Kevin to bow out this early. He'd never miss seeing my father down. He's found a new way of turning the knife,' she laughed, cynically, Kevin's laugh. 'There's a pair of them in it. You just got caught in the middle this time, I've always been there. But I won't forget this.'

That afternoon I cycled down to the back river. The place was deserted. I peered anxiously into the water but it was clear. After that I cycled back to Mullarney, right down the lane. I left my bike at the bridge and crossed to the house. There was a stillness about the place that I'd never noticed before. I went quietly up the stairs. I don't know what I expected but the place was deserted. I was relieved. I sat at the window and looked out on the scorched fields and beyond, to the trees that were turning in spite of the Indian summer.

I don't remember when the idea came to me, some time that night, I think, but I woke up with a clear notion of what I had to do.

'I need the car for a couple of hours,' I told my father.

'Right.'

'Just somewhere I want to check out.'

'Do you want me to come with you?'

I shook my head.

'It's probably a wild idea. I won't be too long. I'll be back before lunchtime.'

I drove through Athy, out the Monasterevin road, my mind racing ahead of me, rehearsing the walk across the bog, rehearsing the moment when I'd look into the pool. On through Kilberry, over the hump of the canal bridge and down the potholed bog road. I parked the car at the belt of trees where we'd left our bikes. I knew it was a wild idea but I had to follow it through.

I tried to run across the bog but the best I could do was to walk fast. The heat of the whole summer seemed to come up from the turf beneath me. The bog-cotton was wilted, the heather fading to the colour of the peat all about it.

I tried not to look at the distant shed. It would never come nearer if I did. I'd walk two hundred steps and then look up, to check my bearings. I thought of the night, walking home from Carlow, when I'd gone ahead of Kevin. I remembered sitting on the pitch and putt gate, seeing him come over Barn hill. And then I counted another two hundred steps and so on until, finally, I was close enough to see the shining sinks and the corrugated slats of the shed wall.

Cutting across the banks of peat-moss, I came out at the side of the pool where we'd gone swimming. I took a deep breath and peered quickly into the water. It was still. And clear. I exhaled and turned to walk away but something stopped me. Intuition. It couldn't have been anything else.

There was nothing to see or hear, not from where I stood, but, suddenly, I knew and terror froze in my belly. It was winter on that sun-baked bog and I was shivering. I wanted to run but I had no idea why. There was nothing to run from, just metal sinks sitting in the morning light, a shed whose open doorway was an inviting shadow. What would I run from? What would I say when I got home? That I ran from the fear of fear? Would I ask someone else to come out here, my father or Kevin's father to walk through the door that I wouldn't darken myself? I couldn't do that.

So I crossed the yards of crumbling peat, the yards we'd covered in a dozen naked bounds a few weeks before and I knew for certain that I'd found him, even before I heard it. The singing of the bluebottles in their song of death.

I scanned the bog for a sign of life but it was deserted, nothing but the light shimmering and the silence of millions of decaying years.

'Nobody but you,' I said out loud, talking myself towards the doorway, pulling my shirt over my mouth and stepping into the lightless shed.

I knew where he'd be. It took a moment to adjust to the shadows and then I saw him, hanging above the small wooden platform. It might have been anyone, a blackened and bloated face, arms that were sticks hanging from a shirt that was Kevin's. That was all I saw, no open eyes, no look of terror or anger or accusation, nothing recognizable. Just a corpse dangling in the heat of a metal shed. I stepped closer. The flies rose from his face like a mantilla and settled again. And then I backed away out of the shed, turned into the face of the light and the sun and started running, feet pounding the soft brown earth, running until I was sick, stopping to vomit and then running again, back to the car, starting the engine before the door was closed behind me, bumping back along the track, the car lurching over the canal bridge and out on to the main road. Driving to the phone box in Kilberry. Ringing the police, ringing my father, waiting at the roadside for the squad car from Athy, the silence of that Sunday morning and then a fly buzzing in the back window of the car and I was sick again.

*

The priest in the hospital morgue, leading the prayers for your soul, as if your soul could be harnessed.

'Our father who art in heaven, hallowed be thy name. Thy kingdom come, thy will be done on earth as it is in heaven.'

And the sounds of the world going by outside, the flow of traffic from the road like water over a dam, there, always there.

'Give us this day our daily bread and forgive us our trespasses as we forgive those who trespass against us.'

Your mother's sobs coming in the gaps between the phrases, dry and low, almost in time with the rhythm of the words. I thought of Kevin in our kitchen, his dry sobbing.

251

'And lead us not into temptation but deliver us from evil, for thine is the kingdom, the power and the glory, for ever and ever.'

And then her cries become less controlled, as though the end of the prayer signalled the end of the world.

'Amen.'

I was strangely removed from that, too. I listened to your mother's crying and I watched your face and felt it had nothing to do with me. Or you. But I was wrong.

*

'It had nothing to do with you or me,' Hannah said.

We were sitting in a corner of Bracken's loft. Below us, people came and went, cars drawing up in the lane, women carrying cakes and sandwiches on plates, big lumbering men bending into the kitchen, a mumble of conversation drifting across the yard.

'How can you say that?'

'Because it's true. If it wasn't this it'd be something else, Tim. That's the way he was going.'

She kissed me and said: 'Fuck me.'

I slid her black funeral dress over her head.

The mourners came and went in the yard below. The sun slatting across the loft the way it had done all summer. And that evening, after the sealed coffin had been brought to the church, when the house was still packed with neighbours, we stole away, down to Mullarney and fucked again, in the room where Kevin had found us. I didn't know what was going through Hannah's head but I wanted to exorcise Kevin from mine. I wanted to lose myself in the sweat and smell of coming. But I couldn't.

Walking home, afterwards, we passed people on the road. They nodded sympathetically but left us to our conversation. If they'd known, would they have been so circumspect?

'It was his doing, Tim. He had it in him from whenever I can remember, always pushing things when he shouldn't have. If he wasn't in the middle it didn't count. And now he is and, I'll bet, he's laughing his smug little laugh.'

'But it was special to him,' I said. 'I can't explain.'

'It was a frigging room in a derelict house, that's all it was, all it is. I'm glad we did it there. That's why I wanted to go back, he thought he could twist everything by doing this, well he can't, not for me.'

'I don't think . . .' I started to say but she cut me off.

'I know what I'm talking about. It was the same for me as him, he just twisted everything and the more twisted things got the more he enjoyed it. That's the truth. I'd fuck on his grave if I thought it would bury him any further.'

'You're hard,' I said.

'Not half as fucking hard as he was.'

But I wasn't convinced. All that night I lay awake. Despite what Hannah said, it had something to do with me. Maybe everything, even. Maybe Kevin was telling the truth when he said I'd done what his father never could, broken him. Nothing else in his life, our lives, had ever driven him even close to this.

In the morning, I found Hannah in the orchard behind her house.

'He was always a good one at hitting the mark when he wanted to,' she said. 'What he did was cruel to everyone. And he didn't give a fuck. It was just something selfish. That's it, Tim, there's nothing more to it, as far as I'm concerned. The end. He's gone, I mean it. It was his choice.'

And I knew she did but I couldn't cut things out like that, I couldn't cut Kevin out. It was all a confusion. What he'd said and done. It rattled in my head that morning, all through the Mass, and on the road out to Coltstown cemetery and, standing across the grave from Hannah and her father, I just knew he'd been as culpable as Bracken.

After the burial, there was lunch, for the family and friends, in the hotel where I'd worked all summer. The head waiter called me aside as we were going in.

'I'm really sorry, what can I say? I'm sorry.'

'Thanks.'

'Give my sympathies to the family. I don't know them but, well, you know yourself.'

I sat with Hannah but we hardly spoke.

That evening, she called for me. I noticed that she'd changed out of her black dress, she was wearing jeans again. We walked down the fields and sat in the clump of trees where we'd been the night she talked about my mother.

'Don't let him get you,' Hannah said.

'It's not as easy as that.'

'It has to be or you'll never be shut of him. It's as easy or it doesn't happen at all.'

But I was right, it wasn't that easy. I don't know where Hannah buried whatever memories she had but I couldn't bury mine. They were all around me. Bracken burning Kevin's clothes in the orchard, his aunt ringing my father to know if I wanted to take digs with her in Dublin, starting college on my own, Hannah coming up one weekend in October to stay with me when, already, we knew we'd never reach one another across Kevin's bones. That was what she said.

It was the last Sunday in September. She insisted we walk to Mullarney, she insisted we go up into the room in the farmhouse, she insisted we make love there and I agreed but, afterwards, I felt the emptiness I'd felt the last time I'd been there with Kevin. It was as though I couldn't love her anymore, I couldn't separate my love for her from what had happened to Kevin, as though I'd let it all run on too long. I hadn't chosen when I should have and now there was no choice at all.

And Hannah came to see that, too.

The one time she came to stay in my flat, we spent the weekend arguing about Kevin.

'He did what he wanted to do,' she said. 'He got you, I told you not to let him get you.'

'I did a lot of it myself,' I said. 'I wasn't straight with him and then I didn't listen.'

'It was just a summer screw around, you said it yourself, it was just an adventure.'

'For me, not for him. For him it was the first league out from land.'

'Are you telling me you wanted to go on screwing him? You could have.'

'It's not that, Hannah. That was nothing.'

'So, what is it?'

'I should have been more careful, about what was important to him.'

'He was the most important thing to him.'

'That's not true. It wasn't always that way. Things went deep with him.'

'And they don't with me.'

'That's not what I'm saying, you're not listening.'

'You're right,' she said, sharply. 'I've listened all my life and I'm sick listening. But you carry on if you want to.'

She swept her coat and bag off the chair and was gone. I let her go.

I rang her later that week and we met the following weekend, when I went home, but we never slept together again and kissed only once, it was as bleak as that.

I missed her, of course I missed her, but there was too much grief and confusion in my head to leave room for any real sense of the loss of Hannah. And, I think, there was too much anger in her heart for her to allow Kevin or me back into it then.

The following Easter, she gave up her job in the factory and moved to England. Bracken hung on for another six

years and then he died. I saw Hannah at the funeral, shook
her hand, said I was sorry for her troubles. She stayed
around for a couple of days and then she gave the farm to
an auctioneer, for letting.

*

*'Did you do anything about that field?' you asked, last
Easter. 'We really could get moving if we knew we could
get it.'*

'I'll write and enquire,' I said.

*And I did. I got Hannah's address from Des Robinson.
She was living in Birmingham. I wrote and asked if she
was interested in selling the field. I didn't know if I'd ever
hear from her but a letter came a fortnight later, telling
me she'd be home in May and she'd discuss it then,
sympathizing on my father's death.*

*'We might get it then,' you said, when I showed you
her letter.*

'Well, she doesn't say no.'

'Be charming,' you said.

'I'm not sure charm will be enough but I'll try.'

*I thought of telling you the story then but, like so many
things in my life, I didn't.*

*That night or the night after, we were in bed, making
love and your face was buried in my hair, your body on
mine, fucking me in the abandoned way you sometimes
did, repeating my name over and over as if it was the only
thread that held you to me and, out of nowhere, the
thought came that in all our years together, as children*

and young men, Kevin had never once called me by my name, never used it to my face, not even in moments such as this.

I lay there and soaked up the sound, not because it was my name, not even because you were the one saying it but because of the intimacy it wove between us.

*

One afternoon, early last May, I got home from school to find an English registered car in the yard. It was empty. I opened the back door and left my books and copies on the kitchen table and then I saw Hannah, coming around the wall from the old orchard.

She'd changed, though not a lot. Her face was rounder, her hair a slightly different shade but her smile was the same, crooked and mischievous.

'Hello stranger,' a slight accent, but it had been ten years.

'Welcome home.'

She came up the step and I hugged her. She kissed my cheek.

'The place has changed.'

'A little.'

'The shed is gone and I see you've put in another orchard. Going into fruit farming, are you?'

'Not so much me,' I said. 'My girlfriend.'

'Ah,' she nodded.

'Coffee?'

'Yeah, sure.'

She wandered across the kitchen. 'God, this house hasn't changed. You've kept it beautifully. No plastic kitchen units or that crap.'

'No.'

'I was down home, it's collapsing, rotten. The damp.'

'I look in when I'm passing,' I said.

She nodded.

'How's school?'

'Fine, grand, they're nice kids.'

'And the girlfriend, is she a teacher?' she grinned.

'Not really. She was a pupil.'

'Bloody hell. What age is she?'

'Nineteen.'

She shook her head, laughing.

'She's in college,' I said. 'Studying horticulture.'

'Déjà vu.'

I smiled.

'And you're happy?'

'Really happy.'

'Good.'

I poured the coffee and we sat at the table.

'You look great,' I said. 'What about you? What's your story?'

'I have two kids, girls. They're four and three. I manage a clothes shop. I used to be married but I'm not any more, not for the last two years. That's it, really.'

'Makes my life sound dull.'

Hannah smiled into her coffee cup. 'I doubt it.'

'Well, it's good to see you.'

'Last time was at my father's funeral.'

I nodded.

'And the times before that. God, it seems like so long ago.'

'I suppose it does.'

'I went up to the graveyard. I hadn't seen the stone since my father's name was put on it. Just mine left to add, now. But I'm not planning on being there for a while,' she brightened.

'Good.'

'And your dad is gone. He was a nice man.'

'Yeah.'

We drank our coffee in silence.

'How long are you over for?'

'Just a few days. I came on Sunday. Back tomorrow. I'm going to Dublin tonight, getting the early boat in the morning.'

'You'll stay for dinner then.'

'Okay, that'd be nice. Thanks.'

While I cooked, Hannah filled me in on her life. We talked about the farm, she was thinking of selling it, that was the main reason for her visit.

'Probably in September, that's when the lease runs out. But you can have the field if you want it, I told the auctioneer it was a separate issue. Three grand.'

'It's worth a lot more than that.'

'Yeah, well . . .'

'Thanks.'

'I told the auctioneer to draw up a contract in September, when the lease runs out. Is that okay?'

'Of course. But I can pay you soon. I can get a bank draft next week.'

'Time enough when the time comes.'

'Thanks, again.'

We sat over the meal for a long time, reminiscing about the village and the things that had changed and the things that hadn't.

'Maureen Broderick is still going strong, I saw her on the Square.'

'Yeah,' I said. 'And Jimmy. Still part of life.'

Hannah put down her knife and fork.

'Is Kevin still part of your life?'

'Not as much as he was, not really. I still think about him, I still go over to the grave when I'm at a funeral in Coltstown. Do you know, Hannah, it struck me, just a few weeks ago, that I never heard Kevin use my name, in all our years. I don't think he ever did.'

She nodded. 'Probably not.'

'Do you think of him?'

'Sometimes. I still feel the way I felt, you know. If it hadn't been there and then it would have been somewhere else. It'll sound cold to you but I'm sure he would have been pulled out of the Thames or the Liffey or somewhere in the end. I think he was born with that inside him. Fate or some such. I don't think even my mother could have kept that at bay, we certainly couldn't. Maybe you just tried harder than anybody else.'

'Thank you.'

She looked at me.

'I know what you're thinking,' she said. 'His life was rough. It was. They all are. Anyway, it's over.' And then her tone softened and she said: 'The thought crossed my mind, a couple of times, as to what would have happened to us if it hadn't fallen apart at the time. I resented that, the way Kevin seemed to get you even after he was gone.'

'Maybe because he was gone. We were all a good deal younger.'

'That might be it,' Hannah said but she didn't sound convinced.

It was well after ten when she left.

'Drive safely,' I said. 'I'll be in touch and thanks, again.'

I kissed her and then she was gone, sweeping up the lane, red brakelights at the corner and a distant beep of the horn.

*

I remember your excitement the following weekend. We'd walked out into the lane. I stopped at the gate of the field and leaned over it.

'It's yours,' I said.

'What?'

'It's yours. Hannah was here on Wednesday. She said we can have it.'

'What? How much? Are you having me on? You are.'

'I'm not. She said we can have it from September, that's when the lease runs out. Three grand.'

'Are you serious? Jesus, brilliant,' and you hugged me.

'I was very charming.'

'I don't want to know,' you laughed, clambering over the gate and running out into the middle of the field, twirling round and round. 'Brilliant, brilliant, brilliant.'

That was six months ago but I still remember the brightness of your face, glowing in the early summer wind. You spent that whole weekend doing plans for the greenhouses in the field, running out, like a child, to the gate and looking along the line of the ditches. That night, in the pouring rain, you took a flashlight and went out to walk around the headland. I could only sit and smile at your happiness.

'I'll make it work,' you said, when you came back in.

'I know you will, I have no doubt.'

And the afternoon, five weeks ago, when the contract arrived in the post, you were like a child all over again.

I was painting the kitchen when you came in with the letter.

'We have to celebrate this properly,' you said, when you'd read it. 'We have to go out to dinner. I'll go home and get dolled up. I want to tell them at home. This is just brill. How am I going to get through the next year in college with this waiting for me? I can't wait to get working there.'

The words were flooding out of you, you kept opening the contract and rereading it.

'I'll run you home,' I said.

'No, you finish that and get cleaned up and pick me up

*at seven. I'll ring and book somewhere in Carlow. Yes.
Yes. Yes. I never thought I'd see this. Arrrh, I love you.
Wait till my dad sees this. I'll just hand it to him and say
nothing.'*

*You went to change into your jeans and then you spent
five minutes looking for a scarf, the one I found caught at
the foot of the bed. I think about that now. About how
things might have been different if you'd stayed in your
shorts, if you hadn't been looking for that scarf to tie up
your hair. I think about how the mundane can become
electric with significance. I think about this all the time
but it does no good, it never changes one iota.*

*And I think of how, in the end, you cycled away and
left me painting and I saw that you'd left the contract and
letter from the auctioneer on the kitchen table. And I
imagined you arriving home, breathless with the news but
without the letter to hand to your father. I got into the car
and set out after you, leaving the kitchen windows open
and the door unlocked.*

*There were two magpies on the wall at the top of the
lane. I remember that. I stopped in the village and bought
the only bottle of champagne I could find. You'd be
pleased with that, I thought.*

*I put it on the back seat of the car and drove out the
Athy road. I saw the white Cortina ahead of me, skewed
across the road. I saw the lorry behind it, the cab door
open. I saw two men kneeling in the road and then I saw
the bike and then one of the men turned and ran towards*

me, flagging me down. And then I saw your body on the grass verge at the roadside.

*

I wrote to Hannah, the day after the funeral. It seemed the easiest thing to do. A business letter. Explaining what had happened, telling her I'd take the field if she liked but that I knew the farm was coming up for auction next month and that the field would be much more valuable as part of it.

She rang me, the following weekend, to sympathize, to say she'd do whatever I wanted about the field. I told her to sell it.

*

So there it is, such a simple story when you hear it all like that. So many mistakes made and such obvious ones. Such a great part of our lives wasted, all of us. But I've told you everything. Much of it you already knew. Or did you? I find it difficult to be certain about anything these days. Sometimes everything is clear and sometimes I have no way of separating what I said from what I think I said. Maybe, some of it I told for my own sake, to remind me of you but some of it I should have told you a long time ago. Anyway, I tried to make it true. I survive the days in school. I don't look down dim corridors or stay too long in empty classrooms. And in the evenings I have my ritual, watering the trees, your trees last of all before I come inside. I listen to their branches settling, their fruit hanging heavy. I think of my father kneeling in the kitchen, when I was a child, after we'd finished our night prayers. He had a litany of people to remember, sick, dying, dead. I have my litany now. I say it in the orchard while the water lakes around the trees.

Your whisper at night in bed, the way you loved my hands on your face, the way your eyes were blue, then green, the musk of your hair, your voice saying 'I think I'm in love with you', the letters you left, letters I can no longer bear to read.

My litany changes night by night. I remember other things. Sometimes you're my saviour and I have faith in you, in us, and then my litany becomes a creed.

And sometimes there is nothing to believe in and I see that the only thing stringing all of us together is the domino of loss. Maybe Kevin was more right than he knew, people weave and warp our lives so much without even being here. I think of my father in his big brass bed, aching for my mother. And I think of how I wish you'd known him. I think of Kevin. But, most of all, I think of you. And the procession of loss continues and sometimes I believe nothing can bring it to a halt.

Have I talked enough about the past, my love? Can you see now why I was so reticent to talk about it at all? Yesterday I had that intimation, the rainbow buried in the field near Kilkea Bridge. And a dream came. And this afternoon, when I'd finished school, I lit a bonfire on the headland of your orchard, hedge clippings and deadwood, *and suddenly the rain came, the first rain in months. I stood there, letting it wash some of the anguish of the summer from my face. And, then, the flames began to melt from orange to grey and I came up here and sat at our window.*

The air is sour with the smell of rain and smoke. I love that smell. I have hope, at least for now. I think I'll sleep. And wait for you.